Author's Note

This book contains many words and phrases in languages other than English. A glossary has been provided at the back of the book.

This Book is dedicated in loving memory of:

Anne and Frank Shook
Thomas Richard Shook
Gerti and Alfred Strauss
Susan Strauss Lipschutz

SEARCH FOR THE SACRED SCROLL BOOK 3

THE SAMARITAN BONE BOX
MARK LESLIE SHOOK

Newhouse Creative Group

NCG KEY

Search for the Sacred Scroll Book 3: The Samaritan Bone Box
By Mark Leslie Shook

NCG Key
Orlando, Florida
NewhouseCreativeGroup.com
©2024, Mark Leslie Shook

Names: Shook, Mark Leslie
Title: Search for the Sacred Scroll Book 3: The Samaritan Bone Box / by Mark Leslie Shook
Description: Orlando, FL | NCG Key, 2025. | Series: Search for the Sacred Scroll | Summary: A Jewish U.S. Marine sergeant and his Chaplain, a female, carrier-based Navy Rabbi, decipher an ancient code that leads to the discovery of an "original" Torah, hidden for 2,500 years.
Identifiers: ISBN 978-1-945493-78-2 (paperback)
Subjects: LCSG: Jewish. | Thriller. |Adventure. |
Classification: LCC 628.J47.S56 Sea 2025 (print)

"It is...clearer than the sun at noon that the Pentateuch was not written by Moses, but by someone who lived long after Moses." – Benedictus Spinoza, *Tractatus Theologico-Politicus, 1670 CE*

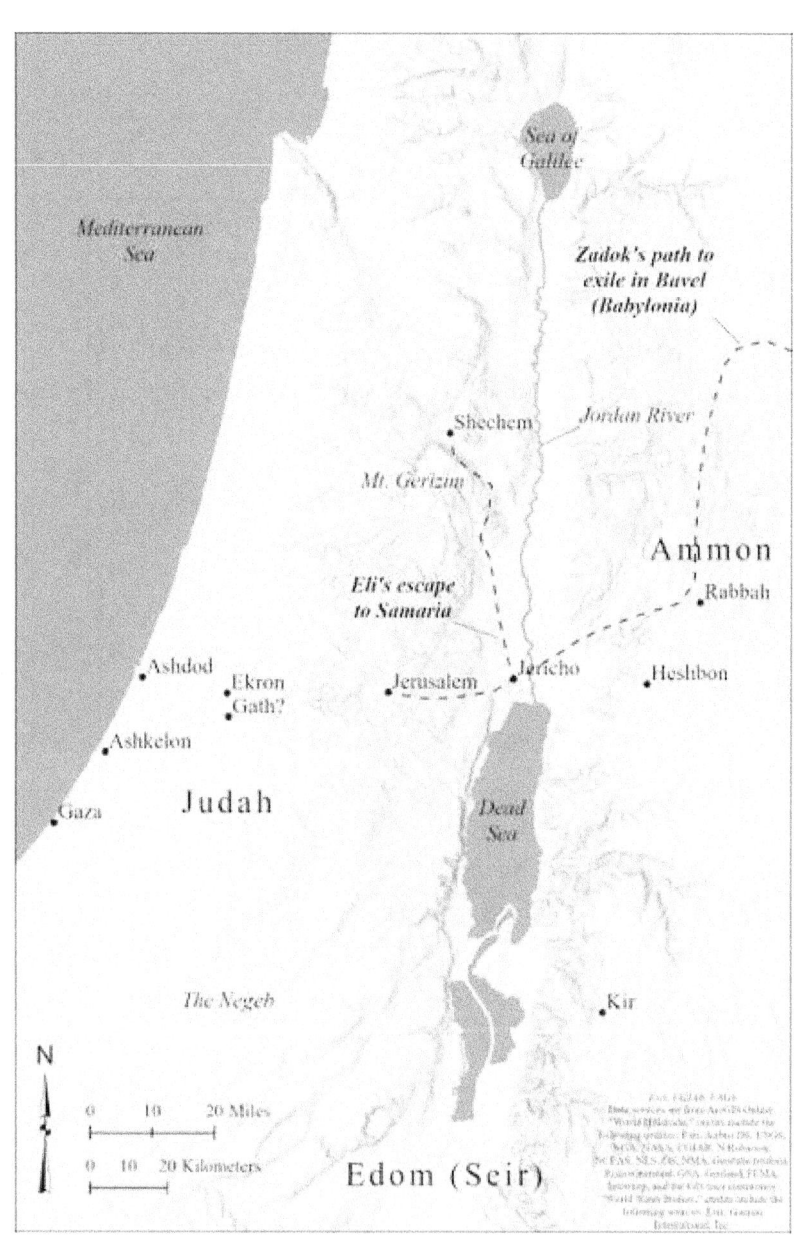

Map by Matthew Thomas

Map by Matthew Thomas

CHAPTER ONE

DATE: March 18, 2009
TIME: 6:15 P.M. Local Time
PLACE: The Carleton Hotel, 10 Eliezer Peri Street, Tel Aviv

Shlomo Malik moved as fast as his eighty-year-old heart, lungs, and legs would carry him. It had been only minutes since Ron Keller was on the receiving end of a pipe bomb tossed from the beach level exit door of the Carleton Hotel. Sucking for air when he reached Keller, Malik placed his hand on the young Sergeant's neck to check for a pulse.

"*Baruch hashem*!" he cried, rolling Keller's inert body over to begin CPR.

Twenty meters down the beach, Navy Chaplain, Rabbi, Lt. J.G. Abby Stone was in the grasp of two medics. "I am not injured!" she insisted, but the two medics held her fast by her arms and dragged her to the nearest of the three ambulances on the scene. "There is nothing wrong with me! Let me go! I have to check on Sergeant Keller. He is the one who needs medical attention, now! Please!"

"Calm yourself, *Giveret*. We will take good care of Sergeant Keller, but we must get you off the beach, for your own safety. We cannot protect you out here."

Stone repeated her pleading in Hebrew as she looked around at the gathering crowd, the pulsing of emergency lights, the constant camera flashes from crime scene photographers, the dozen or so evidence techs in white overalls. The scene reminded her of TV cop shows.

As they neared the ambulances, Stone noticed that none bore the colors or markings of *Magen David Adom* (the Red Star of David). Her continuing shrill demands for release were met with silence.

As soon as Stone was lifted into the ambulance, one of the medics climbed inside and took his place on a stool next to the gurney. "For your safety we need to use these straps," he said, while making sure they were cinched tight.

As the ambulance carrying Stone made its way off the beach, Malik shouted, "I need help now! Sgt. Keller is alive!" He pulled his portable radio from his jacket and repeated his demand, then returned to performing CPR.

Israeli paramedics and soldiers came running. A medic shoved Malik aside as they began to clear the area around Keller.

"Hurry, there is no time to lose!" Despite having just met Keller and Stone, Malik had become attached to the two Americans and was completely caught up in their effort to recover the ancient Hebrew scroll Keller had found in Iraq, which he believed might have been written by the Biblical author, Ezra. Whatever the source of the scroll, its value was now ironically confirmed by the violent efforts unleashed to possess it.

Keller kicked his legs. Malik shoved his way back into the fray and tried to support him. Keller attempted to rise to his feet, but the paramedics held him down. Though he had no visible injuries, they wanted to make sure he was not bleeding internally and that nothing was broken.

"Where is Rabbi Stone?" Keller asked when the paramedics were through with their exam.

"Don't worry, Sergeant," Malik jumped in. "She is fine. She managed to bring down two fleeing gunmen with a pistol and is being taken to the Souraski Trauma Center for a proper exam. We'll catch up to her, now that you've been cleared to leave the beach."

Leaning against one another for support, Malik helped Keller walk to one of the two remaining unmarked ambulances on the beach.

"You are in good hands. I am going to consult with my colleagues and will be right back."

Within a minute, another Israeli paramedic, about the same age as Keller, arrived. He took his time examining the Marine from the top of his head to the soles of his feet. Keller grew impatient. "You know this is my second experience with an explosive device in less than a week," Keller said.

"You are joking," the medic said.

Keller shook his head. "Who jokes about explosions?"

The medic frowned and was extra-conscientious in taking Keller through the concussion protocols. Just as the exam concluded, Keller looked up to see Malik walking quickly toward him.

Malik had a thin smile on his lips. "On your feet Sergeant! We have been invited to a tactical briefing. My friends are preparing to round up the bad guys."

"Please join us in the Command Center." Lt. Colonel Lavi's deep voice emanated from the front of the ambulance and though Keller had met the Central Israel Commander of the National Police Terrorism Task Force just a day before at the Souraski Medical Center during the investigation of the tea shop bombing, it brought him up short.

Lavi pointed at a massive blue bus now parked on the lot of the ice cream parlor. "Let's take this conversation inside."

Keller cleared his throat and was about to speak when he glanced in Malik's direction. Malik shook his head slowly from side to side. Keller reconsidered, then started walking toward the Command Center. Four heavily armed security officers stood by a narrow opening in a movable security fence. The barricade surrounded the Command Center in a circle about ten meters out. When they spotted their commander approaching, they stood aside. Malik and Keller followed Lavi and climbed the steps at the rear of the bus and entered.

In the center of the bus was a large table that could accommodate four persons on each side plus two more at each end. Keller was surprised to find two recent acquaintances in full tactical gear.

Lavi nodded to Keller. "I believe you already know our colleagues, Rafi and Omar."

Keller offered a wan smile to the two SHIN BET operatives who had been called in to advise Lt. Col. Lavi about the first attempt on Keller's and Stone's lives. "Can we just get on with this so I can tell Rabbi Stone that I am still alive."

Lavi nodded and retrieved a small box from the counter at the rear of the bus. Lifting a nine-millimeter pistol from the box, he removed the ammo clip and racked it to clear a remaining bullet in the chamber. Then he picked up a white plastic zip tie, inserted it through the barrel and closed it in a loop.

"Rafi has made me aware of his gift to you. I suppose I should thank you and Rabbi Stone for making sure that the criminals did not get away. But I am now faced with a mountain of paperwork. Before I turn those reports in, I will have to make sure my narrative of the incident makes some kind of sense out of an American Naval Officer killing one criminal and wounding another with a weapon provided by our security service." He sighed. "It's a fine mess." He pushed his hand into his windbreaker and pulled out another handgun. He held it out to Keller. "I will have to keep the gun involved in the shooting but, since I believe that you and Rabbi Stone are still in danger, take this Baretta as a replacement. Take good care of it. It's one of my favorites."

Malik spoke up. "Might I make a suggestion, Colonel?"

"Of course, Professor."

"Why don't you write this up as a tribute to the bravery of our two agents, Yael and Gidon, who were gunned down by the criminals. Tell the press that, while making the ultimate sacrifice with their lives, they were able to bring down two of the criminals? It might bring some peace to their parents."

"I can do that, just so long as you are able to make sure that all this forensic evidence being gathered here gets lost, permanently."

"At my age, I am an expert at losing things," Malik replied.

"Enough with the creative writing class. Let's focus on what comes next."

Rafi pulled a thick sheaf of folded paper from the front of his body armor.

"What is that?" Keller asked.

Rafi carefully unfolded the packet. "It's a diagram of the fifth floor of the hotel, showing the room layouts and exits."

"What are we planning to do?"

"You, Sergeant, are going to do nothing but follow my orders. Two of our soldiers have already died in this operation. Do you understand what I am saying?"

"Yes, but nothing that happened on the beach is my fault!"

Omar broke in with an edge to his voice. "We would not be here at all were it not for the scroll we are trying to recover."

"My apologies. I am very sorry to have brought all of this on you. Just tell me where to go and what to do."

Omar spread the floorplan out on the table. "As best we can determine, the Samaritan leader and one of his lieutenants have barricaded themselves here, in room 502. One of our negotiators has made contact and believes that they are highly agitated but not ready to make any moves against us."

"Then let's go up and storm the room and put an end to all this," said Keller.

Omar shook his head slowly. "We can't. They have the scroll and say that if we do not let them leave, they will burn it to ashes."

"We cannot let that happen," Malik said.

Suddenly, Lavi was on his cell phone. *"Lavi kan."* He spoke rapidly into the phone. Keller had no clue as to what was being said, but sensed a seething anger emanating from the police commander.

"What's wrong?" Rafi asked.

Lavi turned to face Keller.

"Sergeant, we have a problem. It appears that Rabbi Stone has been kidnapped."

"What! How is that possible? You said she was being taken to the Trauma Center for a medical evaluation."

"The Samaritans just informed the negotiators. One of the ambulances on the beach was their getaway vehicle."

Keller was livid. "How could you guys let that happen? I thought your security service was the best of the best. You're worse than the Keystone Cops."

"The Keystone what?" Malik could not look Keller in the face.

Keller's voice rose in volume. "Never mind. What is your *Shin Bet* doing about it?"

"They are, as you say, on the case. It won't be easy to hide an ambulance, even an unmarked one, on the streets of Tel Aviv. The kidnappers know that we have two of their people trapped in the hotel room with the scroll. Despite the threats coming from that room, they do not want anything to happen to the scroll any more than we do. This will give us an opening to negotiate a resolution. Ultimately, I believe they want their people released and will surrender the scroll in exchange for their freedom."

Keller shook his head. "The *Shin Bet* is apparently not the organization I had imagined them to be. We have got to get Rabbi Stone back!"

Malik extended his hands out, palms down, motioning for Keller to calm himself. "We will get her back safe and sound."

Keller shook his head. "I wish I had your confidence."

Stone was unsure of what was happening. It felt as though the ambulance was traveling at a high rate of speed, but she could not hear any siren. The ambulance attendant would not speak with her, no matter what language she tried. After maybe fifteen minutes, she felt the ambulance slow to a standstill and then stop. The attendant stood up. She noticed that the attendant was gripping a syringe in his right hand. In a silent and swift motion, he held her head firmly, turned her to one side and plunged the needle into her neck. Then all was darkness.

PART I: THE RETURN OF THE EXILES

Comfort, comfort my people, says your God. Speak tenderly to Jerusalem, and proclaim to her that her hard service has been completed, that her sin has been paid for, that she has received from the Lord's hand double for all her sins. (Isaiah 40:1-2)

CHAPTER TWO

DATE: The Eighteenth Day of the Fourth Month, In The Forty-Fifth Year Since The Destruction of Jerusalem [540 BCE]
TIME: One Hour After Noon
PLACE: Mt Gerizim, Samaria

Six months had passed since the death of Shoshana bat Talmon, beloved wife of Eli the scribe, loving mother of Gilad, and over-indulgent grandmother to fourteen-year-old Yeshai, a talented scribe in his own right. The three mourners sat beneath the pergola attached to Eli's red brick house, set on a level plateau on the Eastern slope of Mt. Gerizim. A cool breeze came up from the valley below and rustled the grapevines clinging to the pergola. Perhaps at any other time, the trio would have taken pleasure from their surroundings and remarked on the beauty of the day. But this day was a reminder of memory and loss, and their collective silence spoke volumes.

"This morning at sunrise, I went to the burial cave," Eli said at long last. "All that remains are her bones. It is time to prepare the box and gather them together." He exhaled with a heavy sigh, tears welling up in his eyes.

"*Abba*, is there some reason you are in a rush to do this?"

"Why do you imagine I am rushing to gather her bones? Six months have passed."

"It just seems too short a time since her death. I know that you are anxious to finish this task, but is there some other reason for your haste?"

Eli wiped away more tears. His voice was unsteady. "Yesterday, the new Samaritan High Priest came to see me. I sensed a change in his demeanor. I am afraid that our cordial relationship with the Samaritans may have died with your *imma*."

Yeshai was puzzled. "*Sabba*, what do the Samaritans have to do with gathering *Savta's* bones?"

"Nothing and everything, Yeshai. I shall explain all this to you later."

Gilad stood and removed the leavings of their meal from the table. "Let me collect our tools."

A half-hour's walk away from their village brought them to a cave set into a hillside. From faded tool marks and pieces of stone left on the ground near the entrance, it appeared that the opening of the cave had been enlarged to allow people to enter standing up. Across from the opening was a rough-hewn wooden table. A wooden mold in the shape of a box lay on the table. To the side of the table was a stone watering trough, about a cubit in length and a half cubit in width. A stone drinking cup was precariously balanced on the corner of the trough. A small shovel leaned against the trough. A hole in the ground behind the table was the source of the clay to be used in making the box.

The three worked in silence. Gilad dug clay from the hole and placed it into a large, tightly woven basket. Yeshai poured water into the basket and, with his bare hands, began to work the dry clay into a pliant mud. Eli loaded the wet clay into the mold that had served so many other families as the template for bone boxes in their community.

When the clay box was dry enough to hold its shape, Gilad removed the wooden template and placed the newly formed bone box into Eli's hands. Then the three of them walked into the cool, dark cave. Small oil lamps provided enough light to make out the shelves carved out of each of the walls.

"How many people are buried here?" Yeshai asked, noticing the bone boxes lining the shelves.

"Most of our exiled brothers and sisters," Eli responded with a sigh. "We opened this cave almost as soon as the Samaritans allowed us to live among them, a generation ago." Eli nodded to his grandson and tilted his head toward a specific shelf. Yeshai quickly cleared away any dust or debris from a section of the chosen shelf. Together, Eli and Gilad gently placed the empty bone box on that shelf. It would need a week or so to be completely dry.

After two weeks, on another bright morning, Eli announced that the time had come to gather his wife's bones. "I am not sure I can do this," he told his son and grandson. "But we must. Yeshai, go and get the narrow brush and a small pot of ink from my worktable. Before we leave the cave today, I will inscribe your *savta's* name on the box."

Gilad cleared his throat and wiped away his own tears. "Abba, you told me to remind you we have a stop to make before we go to the cave."

Eli nodded. "Indeed, you are right. We must go to the scroll hut."

Yeshai returned with the items his *Sabba* requested, just in time to hear mention of the scroll hut. "*Sabba,* don't you remember? The Sacred Scrolls are gone."

Eli smiled at his grandson. Eli recalled the first time he had entered the small windowless stone shack that stood ten cubits behind the home of the first Judean Priest to be designated Head Priest in the exile. It was about forty years ago. He was twelve years old, and he and his twin brother, Zadok, both apprentice scribes in the Sacred House in Jerusalem, had rescued twenty-four sacred scrolls during the conquest of the holy city by the Bavlim. Uncertain of the future of their people, they divided the scrolls in the hopes that at least some would survive. Twelve scrolls would go into exile in Bavel with the people of Judah. The other twelve would be smuggled out of Judah with Judean *cohanim* seeking refuge in Samaria. At such a young age Eli was made responsible for the safety of the twelve scrolls in Samaria.

"I have not forgotten. It is time for me to show you something more important than the Sacred Scrolls."

"What could be more important than the Sacred Scrolls?"

"Be patient, Yeshai. You will soon understand," Gilad responded..

Eli lit a small oil lamp and handed it to Yeshai. "I want you to enter first," he said.

Yeshai had never been in the hut before. He was surprised by how cool it was inside.. It took a moment for his eyes to adjust to the darkness. Gradually, the glow from the lamp was sufficient for him to make out the details of the interior. The stone walls were thick. On the wall to the left of the entrance, he saw three shelves. He was able to make out four scrolls side by side on each shelf. When he looked closer, he saw the scrolls were tightly rolled, each tied with leather chords. "Abba, I thought the Sacred Scrolls were gone," he muttered.

Gilad placed his hand on Yeshai's shoulder. "These are copies, my son."

"*Sabba*, I have read and studied from copies like these. Why are these guarded? Where are the real Sacred Scrolls that you rescued?"

Eli stood by the shelves and gently touched a scroll. "The Samaritans have the real ones. You were with me that day when I was forced to turn them over to the Samaritan High Priest."

"I never understood why you did that. You were supposed to be the guardian of the scrolls."

"I had no choice in the matter. After the death of your Samaritan grandfather, Talmon ben Aram, too many Samaritans became uneasy about the presence our small Judean priestly community. My marriage to your grandmother did not make us Samaritans in their eyes. To the Samaritans, we would always be Judeans, and they feared that the governor of Bavel would accuse them of harboring Judean rebels. I turned the scrolls over to them to save our people, and the content of the original scrolls. I made a pact with the Samaritan High Priest."

"You mean like a peace treaty?"

"Yes. We gave the Samaritans possession of the Sacred Scrolls. They in turn promised not to expel our Judean community."

"Is that really why the Samaritans wanted our scrolls?"

Gilad laughed. "They wanted God on their side. Your *sabba* believed they were going to create their own version of our sacred stories, but from a Samaritan perspective."

Eli nodded in agreement. "And then they would destroy our Sacred Scrolls."

"Why?" Yeshai asked.

Eli bit his lip. "So that no one could claim there was another version or tell the story from the Judean perspective ever again."

Yeshai stared at his grandfather. "Was there nothing you could do to save the scrolls?"

Eli looked down at the floor and remained silent.

Gilad raised his voice. "Do not speak with disrespect. Your grandfather had no choice. It was the scrolls or another exile for our people."

"So, we lost our scrolls?" Yeshai looked sad.

"Not exactly," Gilad said.

"What is that supposed to mean?"

"Your grandfather had exact copies of the scrolls hidden away. Using these, he reworked the contents of the twelve scrolls into a single, unified Judean scroll, before the Samaritans could finish one of their own."

"So where is *Sabba's* scroll?"

Gilad stepped away from Yeshai and moved toward the hut entrance. He placed his right hand on the shelf support post closest to the door. With care he moved his hand downward, feeling for something on the back of the post with his fingertips. With his hand just above the first shelf, he stopped.

"Give me your quill knife, Yeshai."

Yeshai removed the knife from the side pocket in his robe. It was as long as his hand was wide. Protected by a thin leather sheath, it was a razor-sharp flake of flint bound into a notch in a polished piece of olive wood. The flake was honed at the edges but was not thin down its center. It would not break easily. This was fortunate, because Gilad took the knife and started using it to scrape along the backside of the post. Suddenly, a small section of the post surface popped out onto the shelf, revealing the post to be hollow.

"What is that?"

"Be patient, Yeshai, and you shall see." Gilad handed him back his knife.

Gilad then reached his fingers into the opening and slowly withdrew a tightly wound, leather-covered scroll. It was almost the same thickness as all the Sacred Scrolls combined. He moved aside two of the scrolls on the center shelf to make room for the hidden scroll, untied its binding, and unrolled the scroll within.

"It is time for you to read, Yeshai."

Yeshai was puzzled. "I thought we were going to place *Savta's* bones in the box?"

Eli broke his silence, weeping as he spoke. "It is more important that you read and learn from this scroll before we gather her bones together. It is what your beloved *Savta* would have insisted upon. You will understand why when we finally do gather her bones. We will fulfill our obligation to your grandmother when you have finished reading this scroll."

With that, Eli turned and left the hut. Gilad followed, closing the door behind him.

Yeshai felt abandoned, but only for a moment. He was excited by the prospect of reading a scroll he had never seen before. He grasped the scroll, sat down on the floor of the hut and unrolled a column of the parchment, resting it upon his knees. "What does this all mean?" he wondered.

Yeshai's eyes settled on the very small letters. The text was not from one of the Sacred Scrolls. If it had been, he would have had an easier time reading it. Slowly, he started to sound out the words before him. When his muscles became fatigued, he would walk to the door and step outside to stretch, noting the position of the sun in the sky to track his time in the hut. He could not bring himself to stop reading, despite his growing aches and pains. And then, the reading became familiar. He was reading words he had memorized long ago from the twelve Sacred Scrolls.

In all, it took Yeshai two full days to read the complete scroll. When he finished the task, he was exhausted, exhilarated, and completely transfixed by the stark simplicity of the last words of the scroll:

> *There would not again in Israel arise a prophet like Moses who knew The*
> *Eternal One face to face, witnessing all the signs and wonders The Eternal*
> *One performed in the land of Egypt, before Pharaoh, his servants and his*

entire land. And for the mighty hand and the great and awesome deeds which Moses performed before the eyes of all Israel.

The very next day, shortly before noon, Eli, Gilad, and Yeshai gathered inside the burial cave. They stood around the shallow oval pit that six months and two weeks earlier received the linen wrapped body of Shoshana bat Talmon. At the time she had been laid to rest, fragrant branches from a cedar tree had been gently laid on top of her. With the passage of time, the cedar branches had lost their fragrance, and the linen shroud had disintegrated. Only the disarticulated bones that once were Shoshana bat Talmon remained.

Eli spoke with quiet authority. "Gilad, hand me the *Sefer Torat Moshe,* the scroll of the teaching of Moses."

To Yeshai's surprise, his father reached into the pocket of his outer cloak and produced the scroll that, but three days ago, was hidden in the scroll hut. He handed it to Eli, who placed it in the bone box.

Eli looked at Yeshai and smiled. "Do not worry. I am not placing the only existing copy of the scroll in this box. I have given an exact duplicate to the priests of Anatoth, for safekeeping. They are the kin of the prophet Jeremiah. They will know your name and the name of our family. If you are ever forced to abandon our homeland, seek out the priests of Anatoth and collect the *Sefer Torat Moshe* before you flee to safety."

Next, with gentle loving care, the three mourners gathered Shoshana's bones and placed them in the box. Wordlessly, Gilad placed the lid on the box and sealed it closed with moist clay from a small jar he had brought for this purpose.

"Yeshai, do you have the brush and the ink I asked you to bring from my workshop?"

"Of course, *Sabba!* Here they are."

With a surprisingly steady hand, Eli inscribed one narrow side of the box with the words, *Shoshana bat Talmon - Eshet Eli ben Achituv Hasofer,* Shoshanna daughter of Talmon, wife of Eli, son of Achituv the scribe.

After giving praise to the Most High for the life of Shoshana bat Talmon, Eli and Gilad lifted the box and placed it on the top shelf of the cave, her name clearly visible. And, as they exited the cave, three generations of Judean Scribes living in exile in Samaria shared a single thought: Who would be the next person to read the *Sefer Torat Moshe*?

CHAPTER THREE

DATE: March 18, 2009
TIME: 8:15 P.M. Local Time
PLACE: Unknown Location in Greater Tel Aviv Area

Stone's head ached as she opened her eyes. She tried to move her hands, but they were still strapped to her side. And, though it was pitch black, she could discern that she was still on a gurney in the ambulance.

"Oh my God, is Sergeant Keller alive? Please tell me, she pleaded. "I can handle it. I just need to know."

When the medics who'd taken her from the beach still didn't respond, she began to panic..

"OK. Have it your way. But I need to hit the head, that is, I need to use the bathroom." Stone repeated her monologue in Hebrew, to no avail.

Stone thought she heard a door latch being opened. The sound was followed by a bright light shining in her face, and finally a few words from the medics.

"You are the one they call Rabbi Stone, yes? How come they call you rabbi? You are a woman, no?" The voice was soft and slow.

"Do you live under a rock?" Stone was enraged. "There are communities in Israel and around the world where women can study and become rabbis. Untie me!"

The voice continued. "Women do not become rabbis or priests in my community."

Stone was sensing something about the speaker's accent. He was not a native Hebrew speaker. The mention of his community gave her an idea.

"You must be a Samaritan. Was it you who nearly ran us off the road? Was it you who tried to blow us to pieces, killing five innocent people in the process? What is your name? What is going on? Why are you holding me against my will?"

The flashlight beam held steady as the doors of the ambulance opened wide. An overhead light in the ambulance was turned on. Stone took stock of her situation. She was indeed securely fastened to the gurney in a seated position. She could now see the source of the voice. Stone tried to memorize details of her captor's appearance. He was dressed in black. With his dark complexion it was difficult to guess his age, but he was of medium stature and he looked like he worked out.

"Professor Carlson was right—you are very smart. Yes, we are Samaritans. We are *Keter Shomron*. You and your friends seem to get in our way every time we are close to taking possession of the scroll. When you and the Israelis arrived at the hotel tonight, we were about to succeed with our mission. Thanks to *Shin Bet,* that exchange was not concluded. Oh, we got the scroll all right, just for a moment, but we also endured a police ambush. The scroll is still in the hotel room and the Israeli police will not let our people leave with it. I believe you Americans call it a "standoff." But truthfully, we have the advantage."

"What does that mean?"

"Your *Shin Bet* friends gave us no choice, Rabbi. We shall exchange your life for the scroll."

8:45 P.M.

"So, what's the plan?" Keller was pacing endlessly back and forth along the narrow aisle in the mobile command center.

Rafi stood next to Malik and held his hands out to hold Keller at bay. *"Savlanut* Sergeant. Once we locate the ambulance carrying Rabbi Stone, we will formulate our next move accordingly."

Keller rolled his eyes in frustration.

"What do you want me to say, Sergeant?"

"I want to feel a sense of urgency pouring out of you. I need to know that you are just as pissed as I am that Rabbi Stone is now a captive of some crazed terrorist outfit."

Omar rose from his seat and pulled down a shade over the large side window in the command center. "And that, Sergeant, is our good news. Rabbi Stone is not being held by Palestinian terrorists. She is most likely in the hands of *Keter Shomron*. Listen up, everyone." Omar opened a telescoping baton from his utility belt and pointed at the window shade, except, it was not a window shade. It was a detailed map of the coastal region around Tel Aviv.

"Here—Holon—is where we know the members of *Keter Shomron* are based,. And here is where we are. Our team is now scouring security cameras in this area." Omar made a large circle with the baton. "We will find them."

"Where do you buy your confidence?" Keller resumed pacing.

Lavi stood and blocked Keller. "Sit down, Sergeant. We have work to do. As soon as we locate Rabbi Stone, we are going to time our breach of the hotel room to coincide with her rescue."

Malik cleared his throat. "Do we know the actual location of the scroll?"

"We have no way to pinpoint it."

Keller stared at Lavi. "Who is going to make entry? Will they be using flash-bangs?"

"I see you have knowledge of such devices, Sgt. Keller," Lavi said. "Members of our entry team will go in first. They have lots of experience in these types of situations."

"My concern is the potential for damage to the scroll."

"And my concern, Sergeant, is for all of the lives in that room."

Malik spoke up. "Of course, that is our first concern, *Chevre*. Then what?"

Lavi stared off into space. "When the hotel room is secured, we will give the go-ahead signal to Rafi and Omar to rescue Rabbi Stone."

Keller stood up. "I want to be there with Rafi and Omar when Rabbi Stone is rescued."

Lavi nodded in agreement. "You may go with them. Professor, you're with me and the hotel room entry team. I need you close by to take charge of the scroll. Oh, and by the way Sergeant, please do not shoot anyone this time."

"I didn't shoot anyone last time. That was Rabbi Stone."

8:55 P.M.

"Is there any chance I could get you guys to let me use a bathroom?" Stone pleaded. "I really have to relieve myself, now!"

"One of my men will accompany you but, Rabbi, we are in an abandoned warehouse in an isolated neighborhood. You can scream until you give yourself a sore throat, but no one will hear you. Do you understand?"

"Yes, of course."

"I am glad we understand one another."

"What is your name?"

"Tsadka."

"Thank you, Tsadka," Stone said as one of the alleged paramedics who nabbed her off the beach walked her toward the bathroom. Stone entered, closed the door, and engaged the flimsy lock. She sat down on the commode and began to assess her situation. Her eyes welled up. She could not stop thinking about Sgt. Keller, wondering whether he was alive or dead.

9:05 P.M.

"Are you positive?" Lt. Col. Lavi was again speaking rapidly into his cell phone. He walked over to the window shade map in the command center and drew a circle around a building on the outer edge of the map, in Holon. Lavi allowed himself a smile, closed his phone, and turned to the people in the command center. "The local police have the ambulance on CCTV entering an abandoned warehouse. We have them boxed in with nowhere to go. Now we shall see what's what."

"Send in the extraction team, on the quiet," Rafi said.

"I'm not sending anyone anywhere until we are on the scene."

Keller was shifting his weight back and forth. "Let's get moving then."

Malik, Keller, Rafi, Omar, and Lavi, left the mobile command center and climbed into two black SUVs parked nearby. Omar was at the wheel of one, with Rafi and Keller on board. They left the beach first. Lavi was driving the other with Malik on board for the short trip to the freight entrance of the hotel.

Lavi barked into his portable radio to the team surrounding the warehouse near Holon. "Our people are at least fifteen minutes out. Hold your positions. Do not engage with the kidnappers. Our team will take command on arrival."

9:15 P.M.

Stone ran the palm of her hand against the wall just to make sure she was not imagining the tape joint. She took her belt off and used the edge of the buckle to cut into the wall along the joint. Stone widened the line then followed its path until a square, about three meters in area, was outlined. It must have been a patch for a previous repair job.

"Hurry up in there!" her escort said.

"Stop yelling at me. I am having a difficult time making things work, if you catch my drift. " As Stone spoke, she pulled from the top and the entire thin piece of drywall gave way, revealing a dark hole with some pipes and conduit. "It's now or never," she thought. She crawled into the hole and felt her way forward. She banged her head on a thin pipe above her but kept moving. She had no idea if this shaft would lead her to safety, but at least she would be postponing her death for a while.

CHAPTER FOUR

DATE: Second Day of the Twelfth Month, in the Forty-Sixth Year Since the Destruction of Jerusalem [540 BCE]
TIME: First Hour of the Second Watch
PLACE: Pumbedita, Bavel, on the East Bank of the River Frat

Flood survivors were still searching for their missing relatives and burying their dead when the new Persian rulers arrived and demanded a gathering of the Judean exile leadership. Fear of the turbulence and speed of the River Frat in flood was matched only by the roiling terror taking hold of the Judeans. Why a meeting now? What more could the Persians want from them after they lost so much to the flood?

Standing close together, the fifty or so men and one woman that presented themselves for the meeting were clothed in rags scavenged from the flood debris. With weary eyes, they gazed at the *Pecha*, the Persian governor, who stood before them.

Memukan the *Pecha* looked them over before speaking. His voice was clear and strong. "As I said this morning, when I introduced myself to you, our emperor seeks to ensure that there will be enough food until the next planting and harvest. His Imperial Majesty, Cyrus of Medea and Persia, has therefore decided to end your captivity. You may return to the land of your ancestors."

The announcement stunned everyone except Yeshuah, the *cohein*. He saw the hand of the God of the Israelites at work and shouted as much. "O Household of Israel, your redemption has begun!"

Others echoed his cry. Some shed tears. Others voiced disbelief and despair that they were again being forced into a long and dangerous journey back to Judah.

The *Pecha* raised his hands to silence the group. When quiet was restored, he spoke again. "In three weeks-time, river barges will arrive from the north," he explained. "They will carry grain and olive oil. They are for you and the rest of the Judeans in Bavel.

The armies of the Persian Empire are assembling a caravan of pack camels from Moab. Whatever you can carry in ox carts and wagons, or load on camels, you may take with you back to Judah. A contingent of our army shall be your escorts and protectors on your journey."

Yeshuah rushed forward and bowed low. "We thank His Majesty for his enormous generosity. Is there any way we can show him our gratitude?"

Memukan signaled Yeshuah to rise. "His Imperial Highness knows that those who receive gifts from his outstretched hand will be loyal and devoted servants. He is rebuilding the temples of the gods of many peoples in gratitude for the victories those gods have given him. He believes that the success of his military campaign in Judah, pushing back the Egyptians, is because the god of Judah favors his cause. His councilors advised him that this is a clear sign that the god of the Judeans wants them returned to their ancestral land. He wants so powerful a deity on his side. Sending you back to your homeland is our Emperor's gift to your god."

"The emperor is wise as well as generous," Yeshuah said.

"Must we all go?"

Heads turned.

The shouted question came from behind the *Pecha*, from Miryam the scribe.

Yeshuah held his breath, fearing the *Pecha* would punish her for impertinence.

To the surprise of those assembled, Memukan answered Miryam's question without annoyance. "Actually, some of you must stay as hostages."

Once again, Yeshuah spoke up. "Hostages? Why?"

An anonymous voice from the assembly shouted, "They need the hostages for laborers here. Maybe they intend us to be their slaves."

Memukan directed his response at Yeshuah. "The hostages will not be slaves. They will be our insurance that Judeans will not revolt against His Imperial Majesty."

"Has the Emperor placed any other conditions on our release from exile?" asked Yeshuah.

Memukan nodded. "You shall have no ruler but Cyrus. You shall have no army but the army of Persia. You shall pay taxes only to Cyrus." He smiled. "There is one exception to this rule. Our Emperor will graciously allow you to rebuild your sacred house for your god. He will permit you to raise money for it from your people."

A weaver who lost his entire family in the flood pushed his way to the front. "Who will lead us?"

Memukan replied, "That will be up to you. That is what you must decide today. But, just to be clear, no one who is descended from your last king in Judah shall serve as a leader of your nation. Cyrus knows that would be too strong a temptation for revolt."

The *Pecha* signaled an officer nearby. He watched silently as this soldier carried forward a number of rough cloth sacks and lay them at the feet of Yeshua. One additional sack was placed in Yeshua's hands. Yeshuah just stood there and stared at the pile at his feet, making no effort to look inside the sack in his hand.

The *Pecha* laughed. "Go ahead, open it. It won't hurt you."

Yeshuah opened his sack with care and peered inside. "What am I supposed to do with these?"

"Including the one in your hand, there are twenty identical blue robes. Pass them out to the nineteen people you select to lead your people with you. His Imperial Majesty desires that all who are chosen by you to lead your people in exile shall wear these robes as a badge of office."

Yeshuah walked among the Judeans, engaging many in brief conversations before handing over the sacks one at a time. Most of the recipients were in their forties, craftsmen with valuable skills, a few successful farmers, a half dozen Levites who earned their living as watchmen and several musicians. Surprising the Persians and the Judeans, he presented the last sack to Miryam.

She handed it right back. "It is not wise to make fun of our emperor. That is what he will think when he learns you handed one of these robes to me, an old woman."

Yeshuah put the sack back into her hands and held it there. "Our people need the strength of the widow of Zadok the scribe. I need you to be my scribe."

Miryam nodded in assent. When she lifted her robe from the bag it slipped from her fingers and dropped to the ground. She looked around as she picked the cloth up. She was not the only one having difficulty with the fabric.

Draping his robe over his shoulders, Yeshuah was amazed at how light the garment felt. "What is this material? It is unlike anything we have ever seen before."

Memukan replied, "It's called silk. I'm told it is woven in a land close to where the sun rises.

For the next hour, The newly chosen Judean leaders debated how they would determine who would stay as hostages. In the end, Yeshuah convinced them to allow the people themselves to choose. There was still great suspicion that the emperor intended to do them harm if they remained, but enough Judeans volunteered to stay in Bavel to satisfy the *Pecha's* condition.

The next issue was raised by a Levite who served in the ill-fated *mishkan*. "What about the sacred scrolls?" he asked.

Yeshuah did not hesitate to respond. "Since the earliest days of our exile, the sacred scrolls were protected by our High Priest, Ezekiel. Ten years ago, Ezekiel ben Buzzi, of blessed memory, placed the original scrolls in a sealed stone jar. Since sufficient copies of each of the scrolls existed then, Ezekiel believed that the originals should be protected, but not available to just anyone. The scroll copies were stored at the school for scribes.

"Just days ago, with my own eyes I watched the flood wash away the school. Two of my brother priests drowned trying to protect the scroll copies. *Achim*, my brothers, how could our beloved High Priest know that a massive flood would destroy most, if not all, of the scroll copies? When the waters of the flood receded, I was the one who found Ezekiel's body on the Western bank of the river, the sealed stone jar on top of him. He died protecting those original scrolls."

Behind the gathered assembly, Miryam spat on the ground and said to herself, "How fitting that the murderer should die saving the original scrolls."

The Levite pressed his questions. "Will the original scrolls ever be returned to Judah?"

"Indeed!" Yeshuah responded.

Miryam had heard enough. She lifted the scribal toolbox and slammed it down hard on the table. The crash shocked the assembled exiles into silence. "The original sacred scrolls cannot return with you now," Miryam said.

"And why not?" Yeshuah asked.

"They cannot go until we have sufficient numbers of copies."

The Levite drew so close to Miryam they were breathing the same air. "So, make new copies. The sacred scrolls must be returned to Jerusalem and the Sacred House. It will be a clear sign to the people that the God of our ancestors has caused our return from exile."

"It's not so simple," Yeshuah said. "So far as we know, Miryam is the only scribe left alive in Pumbedita."

"So let Miryam accompany the original scrolls back to Jerusalem and make copies on the way."

"Do you realize what you are asking? The trek to Jerusalem is a difficult one for the strongest of us. Miryam is nearly sixty years of age. She might not survive the journey. Besides, she is responsible for her young grandson."

Miryam pushed through the standing leaders and raised her voice. "Since you all have decided that I am a feeble old woman, do I get a say in the matter?"

"I never intended to insult you," said Yeshuah. "Of course, you get a say!"

Miryam stepped in front of Yeshua. "You all heard the *Pecha*. We have about three weeks before our supplies arrive, and then we must begin the return. Let us send word up and down the river and see if we can locate additional scribes. If more than three can be found, I shall stay here with my grandson among the hostages. We shall make new copies from the original scrolls. Those copies will be taken to Jerusalem, not the originals. When there are sufficient copies and our people are safe and secure in Jerusalem, and the Sacred House is restored, then we shall bring the originals home."

Yeshua held up his hand. "The wife of Zadok is wise. So, here is what we must do. First, we must begin the search for additional scribes among our people. If we find but five or six, we shall leave three behind to assist Miryam in the copying of the sacred scrolls and training more scribes. The rest of those additional scribes will make the journey with us. They will be needed to establish a school for scribes in Jerusalem."

At that moment, it seemed as though all eyes were on Miryam, who lowered her gaze to the ground. Miryam had serious doubts and thought, "What have I done? How can I carry the weight of our people's future on my worn-out shoulders? Oh God of Sarah and Abraham, give me strength!"

After two weeks, five additional scribes had been located. All of them were from villages upriver from Pumbedita. Three were young enough to make the arduous journey. They learned their craft from Zadok, from a time before Ezekiel's *mishkan* existed. The other two were almost Miryam's age. Their abilities to practice their scribal art were like hers, reduced by stiffening joints and failing eyesight. Miryam convinced Yeshuah that they should not return to Judah. "They will slow the journey down. Here they are essential. Together, we shall establish a school for scribes here and begin the process of copying the sacred scrolls."

Yeshuah was forced to admit that Miryam's plan had merit. He took the idea to the new leadership council. The council agreed.

The river barges carrying provisions for the journey to Judah arrived after four weeks, not three. During the unexpected delay, the Judeans speculated that the emperor had changed his mind. Now, as the barges were unloaded, a sense of confidence began to build. For some exiles, there was even a ray of hope for a new beginning. But many Judeans were refusing to make the journey. They feared for their lives and the lives of their families. The Judean leaders were concerned that their final numbers would not be able to meet the expected quota of returnees. Yeshuah sent Judean recruiters up and down the river to the seven surviving exile communities that once served as ports-of-call for the floating *Mishkan*. He wrote a proclamation to be read to each community, stating that the return was a sign of the power of the God of the Judeans, who reached across the wilderness to bring His people home.

One week after the supply barges arrived at Pumbedita, Memukan the *Pecha* was taking his daily walk among the Judeans to gauge the progress of their preparations for the return to their homeland when he asked Yeshuah about Miryam's whereabouts.

"I wish to see her at her work. Where can I find her?"

Yeshuah directed him to the south side of the Judean encampment. "Look for a ragged black canopy. If there are children learning to become scribes beneath its shelter, there you will find her."

Arriving at the canopy, Memukan watched the children, some as young as five, none older than ten years of age, follow the movements of Miryam's pointed stick as she cut letters in the smooth hard-packed earthen floor of the tent.

"Why do you teach them this Hebrew lettering?" Memukan asked, startling the students and teacher alike. "They will not be prepared for life in the new Empire."

"My Lord, *Pecha*, they are not being prepared to serve the Empire. They are preparing to serve their God, the one whom your ruler has seen fit to honor."

"I hope you will also teach them Aramaic, the official language that ties our empire together. Perhaps your God also wishes to communicate with other nations."

"This is but the first step, your Excellency. Is there something I can do for you?"

"Please step outside for a moment."

Miryam narrowed her gaze. "Why the need for privacy?"

Without giving Miryam an answer, the *Pecha* turned and walked away from the canopy. Wary but curious, Miryam followed him.

After taking a few steps, Memukan stopped and turned to face her. "Your husband's brother, Eli the scribe, has given me a message for you and you alone."

Stunned, Miryam stood motionless, then started to back away from Memukan. "How do you know of Eli and why does he entrust a message to you?"

In response, the Pecha extended his hand and revealed a small scroll secured with a thick black wax seal in his open palm. "Eli's personal seal is on this scroll."

Miryam looked at the seal. "And how would I know his seal from any other?"

"Just look at it. That will be for you to decide."

At the center of the seal, the wax bore the finely engraved image of a lion's head. Beautiful, pre-exilic Hebrew lettering formed the outer edge of the wax. It spelled out "Eliezer ben Achituv."

Miryam broke the seal and unrolled a small piece of sheepskin parchment. Just two words were written in the middle of the parchment. "Trust him."

"Please, I mean no disrespect Excellency. The seal and scroll may be from my brother-in-law, but why are you the messenger? Isn't this task below your station?"

Memukan looked around to make sure no one was within earshot. "I met Eli and his wife Shoshana two years ago when I arrived in Shomron. I was assigned there as a diplomat from our Emperor. Eli was serving the Samaritan chief as his scribe. In time, I was welcomed to Eli's and Shoshana's table. I shared many meals in their home."

"So, you, my brother-in-law and sister-in-law became friends. Is that it?"

Memukan cleared his throat. "More than just friends. I grieved with him when Shoshana died and sat with him and his son and grandson after her funeral. It was then that Eli told me about his twin brother, Zadok, and their regular correspondence. He said the last letter he received from Bavel was written by you. It told of Zadok's death."

Miriam nodded slowly. "This is true."

"Have you not wondered why Eli wrote no reply to that letter?"

Miryam took a moment before responding. "I thought that his grief or the great distances between us caused him to stop."

Memukan took the scroll and seal from Miryam's hand. "He stopped writing to you because it was too dangerous. Shoshana was one of the reasons for Judean safety in Samaria. Since her death, the Samaritans have been treating Eli, his family, and the rest of the Judeans living in Samaria with suspicion. Some were openly accusing him of treason."

"That's ridiculous."

"I cannot take any chances that this seal and scroll might fall into the wrong hands." Memukan dropped the seal to the ground and then crushed it with the heal of his boot. He tore the scroll into small pieces and scattered them to the wind. "The Samaritan leaders suspect Eli's letters to Zadok were really secret plans plotting the overthrow of the Samaritans on Mt. Gerizim in favor of the Bavlim."

"But the Bavlim are gone. There is no threat from them anymore. You Persians saw to that."

"The Samaritans are even more afraid of us than the Bavlim. Afterall, we conquered them so we must be the graver threat. In any event, Eli urged me to attempt to warn you and your people."

"Warn us about what?"

"At one of the last meals I shared with Eli before leaving for Bavel, I revealed to him our emperor's plans to end the exile of the Judeans in Bavel. He was horrified. He insisted that the Judeans in Bavel be warned of the hardships that awaited them in Judah. I became Eli's messenger to you because my imperial duty is to ensure that the emperor's plan for the Judean exiles is successfully carried out. Eli's message to you will help me to fulfill that obligation."

Miryam looked directly into Memukan's eyes. "Since you have arrived here, you have presented our imminent return to Judah as a precious gift from the emperor. You said nothing about hardships."

"That's just it. Eli understood that the return from exile was a gift, but he also knew that it would come at a heavy price. His position, close to the leadership of the Samaritans, gave him a unique perspective from which to observe the push and pull of area tribal chiefs as they all competed for power under the Persian empire."

Miryam became indignant. "We do not seek power. We seek only our safe return to our homeland."

"What you exiles do not realize is that your safe return will depend on the good will of the Judeans already in the land. Fifty years ago, while you and your parents were carried off into exile, Judean farmers and herders were left behind by the Bavlim to fend for themselves. The Bavlim had enough farmers and shepherds of their own in Bavel. They did not need to import more of them. They only sought to benefit from craftsmen and artisans. At first, the ones left behind nearly starved. But they survived and built a life for themselves without your leadership. They might acknowledge that they are your distant kinsmen, but they don't want you back as their new masters."

Miryam shrugged. "We will find a way to reunite with them. I am sure."

"Well, they should not be your only concern. The tribes and nations that surround Judah today, including the Samaritans, don't want you back either. They have been plotting various ways to make sure that returning Judean exiles would never succeed in threatening their hard-won autonomy."

Miryam stiffened. "What tribes? What nations?"

"Phoenicians, Amorites, Ammonites, Edomites, Ishmaelites, and Midianites. They would prefer for you to remain here in Bavel. The Samaritans are especially angry at the emperor for encouraging your people to return and giving you the resources to rebuild your sacred house in Jerusalem. The Samaritans want to be the sole tax collectors and masters of a Sacred House treasury. They want that treasury to be the one that sustains their Sacred House on Mt. Gerizim. Eli wants you to know your people are walking into a trap."

Miryam smiled. "Eli would not send you to lecture me about the dangers of local politics in the Province Beyond The River. What are you not telling me? Why are you really here?"

Memukan shifted his weight from one foot to the other. "Eli wanted you to know that the twelve Sacred Scrolls once under his care are gone."

"What? What do you mean, gone?"

"The new Samaritan High Priest took the twelve scrolls from Eli when his predecessor died. It was shortly after Shoshana died." The *Pecha's* voice was nearly a whisper. "The new High Priest explained to Eli that the Samaritans wanted to make their own copies. Eli wanted you to know that, for the safety of the Judeans living in Samaria, he was unable to refuse this request."

Miryam strained to keep her voice down. "Of what use are the scrolls to the Samaritans?"

"Observing Eli's dedication to maintaining the scroll tradition over the years, the Samaritans have come to understand the importance of these documents to the well-being of the Judeans living among them. Eli thinks they are going to rewrite key passages in the text to elevate the importance of Samaria and the Samaritans at the expense of the Judeans. If they do this, they will have to destroy the original scrolls. Their continued existence would prove the altered Samaritan scrolls to be forgeries."

"None of this makes sense. For many years, Eli wrote to Zadok, praising the unity of Samaritans and Judeans. He explained to us that they worshipped the same God and venerated the Sacred Scrolls. What happened? How did this all go so terribly wrong?"

Memukan stared at the ground. "This is all the fault of our empire. When we began to prepare the Samaritans for the return of the Judeans from Bavel, their attitudes toward any and all Judeans soured. In our obsession with expanding our power, we became entangled in so many wars, we could not always pay attention to the territories already under our control. The Samaritans have been loyal to us, but they also know we are spread too thin. They see our temporary weakness as an opportunity to expand their own reach before your people complete their return to Judah."

"What does my brother-in-law expect me to do about it? I am a widow caring for an orphan."

"Miryam, since I have arrived in Bavel, I have observed your interactions with the leaders of your people. They grumble and complain, but mostly they follow your advice. You have done well to keep the sacred scrolls from returning to Judah. Eli fears that if your people bring them back to Judah, the scrolls will disappear. Your leaders will listen to you. You must tell them to be very careful on their journey home. They must prepare to defend themselves. As Eli said to me, 'The land promised to Abraham will welcome them. The non-Israelite peoples who now occupy its cities and villages will not.'"

Miryam was considering her options when she heard a small voice call her.

"*Savta*! Where have you been? Is our lesson over? Can we go home now?" A young boy grasped her hand and pulled her in the direction of the canopy.

Miryam reached down and tussled the sturdy child's thick, curly hair. "Excellency, permit me to introduce my wise grandson, Hilkiah, great nephew of Eli the scribe. He has asked the essential question of the hour. "Can we go home now?"

CHAPTER FIVE

DATE: March 18, 2009
TIME: 9:25 P.M. Local Time
PLACE: A Warehouse in Greater Tel Aviv Area

The *Shin Bet* surveillance team was well hidden outside the warehouse. Responding to a pre-arranged signal, a member of that team approached Rafi, Omar, and Keller. Cocking his head in Keller's direction, he said, "Who is this guy?"

Rafi responded. "He's OK. You can talk."

The team member held out a small device with a viewing screen so Rafi, Omar, and Keller could see. "The heat sensor shows three bodies giving off a good signature, but the fourth body keeps appearing and disappearing. It is as if it is behind a lot of pipes and junk. It is also on the move. That could be Rabbi Stone."

"Nobody opens fire until we are certain which of the heat signatures is hers," Rafi ordered.

"Are you insane? Those heat sensor things are wrong 50 percent of the time. We can't gamble with Abby's life."

Everyone looking at the video monitor caught the intimacy and lack of military discipline in Keller's use of Rabbi Stone's first name.

"So, what's our next move? Omar asked.

Before anyone could answer him, a very powerful sound system carried Rafi's voice to the kidnappers. *"Keter Shomron,* we know you are in the warehouse. You are not going anywhere. If you harm Rabbi Stone, this will be the day that you all die." His threat could be heard in Beirut.

Rafi then barked out a phone number. "972.36300222. Tsadka, that is my mobile number. Call me. We need to talk, now!"

A full five minutes passed before Rafi's mobile started vibrating. He waited a few moments then answered the call. "So, what's it to be? Surrender or death?"

"All we ever wanted was the scroll. You give us that and the woman goes free."

"It's not that simple. The scroll does not belong to you."

"It is that simple. Free our people at the hotel and bring them and the scroll to us. We want your car with a full tank of gas and an escort to Nablus. Call me when you have it arranged." The phone went dead.

Rafi looked directly at Omar. "Get on the radio. Tell Lavi it's a go! Move in when you are ready."

"No, wait! What's your rush? Rabbi Stone will get hurt, or worse." Keller grabbed Rafi by the arm. Rafi shook him off.

"Sgt. Keller, we have a lot more experience in these things than you do. Back off, now!" Rafi motioned for two police officers stationed nearby to step forward and restrain Keller. "Both the hotel and the warehouse will be breached at the same time. The Samaritans will be waiting for our answer to their demands. We shall overwhelm them, quickly. That is how we save lives."

Keller was not so sure.

9:45 P.M.

Stone heard explosions and gunfire from somewhere behind her and, as dust and debris showered down on her, she could make out a lot of yelling of commands in Hebrew. Stone froze. She did not know where safety was. Should she keep going forward or should she turn around and go back to where she started?

"Rabbi Stone, it's me, Sergeant Keller! You are safe now. The Samaritans are in custody. Come to the sound of my voice."

"Aaron, is that really you?" Stone turned around in the confined space, banging her head once again on an overhead pipe. "Ooowww! I need some light in here so I can see where I am going."

A high intensity work light was placed in the utility space.

"I see the light!" I am coming out."

10:05 P.M.

Neither Keller nor Stone would be the first to let go from the power hug. Both were lost in tears of joy and relief. Keller spoke first. "I was so worried that we would lose you. How do you feel?

"I have a headache. I am not sure whether it is from the drugs they gave me or from banging my head on pipes for the last half hour." Looking at Keller as if for the first time, Stone reacted with a start. "Hold on! How is it that you don't have a scratch on you? I thought you were dead."

Rafi separated the two of them and pushed them toward the waiting SUV. "We are going to meet at the mobile command center on the beach to debrief. We shall find answers then."

Stone raised her voice. "What about the scroll? Is it in our possession? Was it damaged?"

"We'll find out at the debriefing. Let's get moving."

10:45 P.M.

Stone was taking in the details of the interior of the mobile command center. The technology on display was impressive for such a closed space. The whole crew, except for Lavi, was seated at the table. Stone took a place next to Keller and then, below the table, entwined her right ankle around his left. She intended to hold on tight. Keller made no effort to disconnect. Keller spoke first.

"Tell me, Colonel, Professor-Malik, why am I alive?"

"Are you asking for my theological opinion or for my military expertise?"

Keller responded with a harsh tone. "I'm not trying to be a smart ass. I know what a pipe bomb can do. I have seen enough of the shredded bodies left in their wake. I just want to know how it is that I survived a pipe bomb thrown at me."

Stone tried brushing the debris from her once black fatigue jacket, now gray from the thick dust she gathered during her crawl-space escape in the warehouse. The dust did not come off without a fight. "Sgt Keller, please remember we are guests here. No need for raised voices."

Malik stroked his chin and looked at Keller. "It's all right. I understand. The beach sand saved your life. Our bomb techs have not had a chance to do their investigation yet, but the device must have landed on a small dune that was not compressed. The force of the explosion was most likely directed downward into the dune, which absorbed a great deal of dangerous energy."

At that moment, Lavi climbed into the command center, closing the door behind him. He took a moment to survey the table, making sure all of the principals were there. He took a seat at the head of the table. "We have a lot of ground to cover, and it is getting late. To expedite matters, permit me to open the conversation. First, Sgt. Keller. What happened at the back door of the hotel?"

Keller cleared his throat. "I saw a pipe being thrown in my direction from a narrow opening at the door. I hit the deck. That's all I can remember."

Stone took a sip from a water bottle, then coughed several times before she spoke. "First, I owe you all my life. Bless you for coming to my rescue. When the shooting started on the beach, I was acting on pure adrenalin. I saw Sgt. Keller face down in the sand. I thought he was dead. I grabbed his weapon and started shooting at the guys who came flying out of the hotel. I think I emptied the whole clip."

Malik was doing his best Hebrew-accented impersonation of John Wayne. "You shore did. That was some 'mighty-nice' shootin.' You are truly dangerous, Rabbi. I think one of them is dead. The other was wounded in his *tuches.* "

"Let's try to do this in chronological order. What happened in the hotel room with the first attempted take-down? Rafi, you're up."

"Of course. It was all going as we planned it. We got to the hotel room before the Samaritans. There were two of them. They used the key card supplied by Carlson to make entry. We immediately grabbed them, threw them down on the bed, but before we could secure them with zip-ties, the shooting started. Someone in the hallway was shooting into the room using a silencer. Omar and I returned fire and ended up chasing them down five flights of stairs. When the shooters reached the ground floor, they made their escape through the fire doors that opened onto the beach. You just heard what happened after that."

"Did you see the scroll? Where was it?"

"Before the Samaritans made entry, the scroll was secured in the room safe where Professor Carlson left it. We confirmed it was still there, then thought it would be best to leave it right where it was. I became a little preoccupied with a full-on fire fight, trying to save myself, Omar, and the Samaritans. By the time we returned to the fifth floor the Samaritans had managed to barricade themselves in the room and were threatening to destroy the scroll."

Lavi pushed the issue. "How were you able to verify that the scroll was still in the room with the Samaritans?"

Omar took up the narrative. "While you guys were beginning the search for Rabbi Stone, I called the tech guys, and we inserted a fiber optic camera beneath the door to the hotel room. The Samaritans must have opened the safe and taken the scroll out because we could see the shape of a scroll wrapped in a towel, sitting on the desk beneath the window. The Samaritans didn't have the time to remove the scroll from the room. They were still trying to make sense out of who started the shooting."

"Do you know who sent the shooters?" Keller asked.

Omar shook his head and turned in the direction of Lavi. "It's too soon to know for sure. We will know more when Colonel Lavi has a chance to question the one who survived."

I think I recognized that one," said Lavi.

Stone stared at him. "Is that possible?"

"I am fairly certain that the wounded shooter was arrested weeks ago during an undercover operation against a West Bank car theft syndicate."

"Does that mean the shooters were Palestinians?" Keller asked.

Stone pressed the point. "So, you think the Samaritans and the Palestinians hooked up?"

Omar shook his head. "Hooked up? Rabbi, you are getting way ahead of our investigation. We have more questions than answers. Your question implies they shared a common objective with regard to the scroll. We don't know that. When the shooting into the hotel room started, it was very clear to us that the Samaritans were taken by surprise. They started yelling at us to tell our men to stop shooting. When we informed them that all of our agents were either in the room or accounted for, they had a look of real terror in their eyes. They certainly did not act like they were expecting to be freed from our custody by accomplices."

"We need to have a chat with the momma's boy," Malik said.

Keller raised his voice in frustration. "Who's the momma's boy?"

Stone smiled at Keller. "The one I shot in the *tuches*. He was yelling for his *Emah*, momma. While I doubt that he is any kind of mastermind, he might point us in the right direction."

Omar agreed. "I think we will manage to obtain all we need from him with only a brief amount of waterboarding."

"Omar, you can't!" Stone protested.

Omar laughed. "Relax, Rabbi. I was only kidding. You Americans are so programmed to believe the worst about Israel. We are going to have your bullet pulled from his *tuches* at the emergency room. Then we will take him to the Spa for a massage and a facial."

"No, really. What will happen to him?" Stone asked.

"He will be interrogated by our experts. We shall know all that he knows and do it without torture, I promise.

Rafi reached under the command center table and withdrew a small object and extended his hand to Stone. "I think you will want this."

The scroll was still in Keller's Marine-issued towel. Stone handed it over to Keller.

Rafi focused his eyes on Keller. "Now, it is even more precious. It has cost two Israeli lives. Take good care of it. I hope what you learn from it will be worth the cost."

Keller held the scroll in his hand. "So do we, Rafi, so do we."

CHAPTER SIX

DATE: The Thirteenth Day of the Twelfth Month, In the Twenty-Fourth Year Since the Return of the Judean Exiles from Bavel [516 BCE]
TIME: Two Hours before Dawn
PLACE: Mt Gerizim, Samaria

"Yeshai ben Gilad ben Eliezer, wake up! It is time for you to answer for your crimes!"

Yeshai jumped out of his bed, wrapping himself in a thin wool blanket so as not to feel so exposed. He was blinded by the light of a burning torch held close enough to his face to cause pain from the heat. Raising his hands as a shield he saw a familiar face. "Matana? What are you talking about? Why have you broken into my house?"

Behind Matana, Yeshai saw two large men dressed in cream-colored robes, the distinctive garb of the Levites.

The Samaritan leader and Chief Priest cleared his throat. "Are you the guardian of the Sacred Scrolls of Judah?"

"Your Excellency, Matana, why are you acting this way? Who are these Levites with you?"

"They serve in the Sacred House in Jerusalem. Now that the restoration of the Sacred House in Jerusalem is almost complete, they have been sent by their High Priest to take custody of the scrolls you stole."

"Have you been possessed by a demon?" Yeshai asked. "You know that the Sacred Scrolls were not stolen—many years ago, they were rescued by my grandfather from the burning Sacred House in Jerusalem."

Yeshai turned to the Levites. "Yes, as Head Priest of the Judeans in Samaria, one of my responsibilities would have been to serve as 'guardian of the scrolls.' But, as Matana knows full well, they have never been in my care."

The faces of the Levites revealed nothing. Yeshai felt like he was speaking to a stone wall. He turned back to Matana. "Why are you doing this? We grew up together, my friend. We explored the hills and caves of Samaria together. We learned to read and write together. And we were both present twenty-four years ago, when my grandfather handed the Sacred Scrolls over to your father, Amshel. Since that time, you and your priests have had the Sacred Scrolls, not my grandfather, not my father, and certainly not me."

A large open hand connected with Yeshai's face, knocking him off his feet. "*Shakran*-Liar! Answer the Samaritan. Where are the Sacred Scrolls?" The taller of the two Levites was shouting.

Yeshai cast a pleading look at Matana. "Why are you letting them do this? You know the truth."

Matana shook his head. "Yeshai, for your own good, stop with the lies!"

The Levite who struck Yeshai repeated his demand. "Tell me where you have hidden the scrolls? Return them to us now and we shall be on our way back to Jerusalem."

Yeshai tilted his head toward Matana. "They have the scrolls."

"We do not! They are of no value for us."

But Yeshai knew better. He had heard from some of his former Samaritan students that they were hard at work making changes to the Sacred Scrolls, eliminating references to Judah and the Judean priesthood and elevating the importance of Samaria and the Samaritan priesthood. "I do not have the Sacred Scrolls," he cried one last time, though he realized that protesting his innocence was futile. The security of the entire Judean community living in Samaria depended on the good will of the Samaritans. He could not place his people in peril by trying to expose Matana's lies.

"Then we have no choice but to bring you back to Jerusalem. Get dressed."

In the shadows cast by the torch, Yeshai gathered his priestly headcover and tunic from a shelf, along with a worn pair of sandals. When he was dressed, he looked into the eyes of the taller of the two Levites. "What is your name?"

"My name is Calev."

"Calev, am I permitted to ask you a question?"

Calev raised his eyebrows.

"Your fellow Judeans returned from exile in Bavel more than twenty years ago. In all those years, your leaders have never once come to Samaria and asked us about the Sacred Scrolls. Why now?"

"The question you asked is worthy of an answer," Calev said as he fastened heavy iron chains around Yeshai's wrists and ankles. Laughing, he added, "Ask the High Priest when you see him in Jerusalem."

As he watched the horse-drawn cart carry Yeshai away, Matana ben Amshel breathed a sigh of relief. Yeshai had been telling the truth; Eli, his grandfather, had turned over the scrolls to the Samaritan leaders years ago. But Matana believed that concealing the truth about Samaritan plans for the scrolls protected his own community from the wrath of the politically powerful returnees from Bavel. The Judean returnees were now the favored vassals of Persia in the region. Matana sensed that Yeshai was in chains because the Judean High Priest needed information from him; information that only he possessed.

Yeshai pushed himself up to a seated position and stared at the winding road in front of him. His view of the hills of Judah was obstructed by the iron bars that confined him. What he did see through the bars were untended fields colored a light shade of green, the result of abundant winter rain. A few hardy yellow and purple flowers pushed their way through the green, sure signs of the spring to come.

The first few hours of the rough and tumble journey to Jerusalem gave Yeshai ample time to ponder his situation. *Matana said I would 'answer for my crimes.' But what crimes have I committed?*

Yeshai's eyes welled up. "Eternal One, are You sure I am the one to lead your *cohanim* in Samaria? If only I had the wisdom of my grandparents, Eli and Shoshana, or the strength of my father, Gilad, I could fulfill Your purpose. But You saw fit to take from me everyone I loved."

Yeshai's mourning seemed without end. First Baruch, his only child, three years old, died after a prolonged fever. Then his dear wife, Nechama, succumbed to the same fever. When his father, Gilad, the Head Priest of the Judeans in Samaria, died, Yeshai was not permitted to grieve in the Judean manner, surrounded by family and friends. An hour after his father's body was laid to rest in the communal burial cave, the council of Judean *cohanim* in Samaria showed up at his home and elected Yeshai as his father's successor. According to the traditions of the Judeans in Samaria, this meant he was also the sole guardian of the Sacred Scrolls. Yeshai laughed out loud as the cart swayed from side to side. He was the condemned guardian of the Sacred Scrolls, now in the hands of the Samaritans. But there was indeed a secret destined to die with him. He was now the only one left alive who knew where the *Sefer Torat Moshe* was hidden.

CHAPTER SEVEN

DATE: March 18, 2009
TIME: 11:30 P.M. Local Time
PLACE: #24 Jabotinsky Street, Tel Aviv

Malik, Keller, and Stone made the brief trip from the mobile command center at the Carleton Hotel to Malik's home in silence. Upon arrival, Malik secured the ancient scroll in a safe hidden beneath his refrigerator. Their growling stomachs reminded them they had not eaten since that morning. The trio decided to make do with a meal from Malik's pantry. It was more breakfast than dinner. Nevertheless, the fresh bread and strong coffee pushed away their fatigue.

After cleaning up, Malik pulled the drawstrings on the kitchen garbage bag and walked to the back door.

"Where are you going?" Keller said.

"Where does it look like I'm going? You see, this is garbage and what we do with it is put it in the garbage can at the back of the house so the rats and cats can battle all night for their share."

Keller started walking towards the kitchen door. "I'm coming with you."

"I'll be fine, Sergeant. Relax. We have all been under a great deal of stress. I realize that we all might respond with hyper-vigilance, but we need to keep from overreacting. For the moment we are safe. It will take a day or so for the Samaritans and their backers to figure out their next move. Meanwhile, we need to use this time to find answers to some key questions. We need to know why that scroll was written and what it contains beyond Psalm 137?"

When Malik re-entered the kitchen a moment later, Stone greeted him with a challenge. "Professor, do you think we have the ability to reveal the scribe's purpose in writing the scroll?"

"God willing." Malik secured the back door. "The scroll has endured the wars and upheavals of the Near East for at least two thousand four hundred forty-nine years. That alone makes it a worthy object for intense investigation."

Keller smiled. "That is, if it is not some colossal fake."

"Sergeant, you found it sealed in a *geniza* behind a wall in Fallujah. Why? Why did the Jewish community of Fallujah take such care with it?"

"How do you know the *geniza* was within the Jewish community?" Stone asked.

"Rabbi, I was born there! Keller said the *geniza* was in the middle of the Al Jolan neighborhood. That was the Jewish quarter of Fallujah. I am excited by your discovery of Psalm 137 because it was written four centuries before the Dead Sea Scrolls became ink on parchment. I am even more excited by the prospect that the scroll is of greater significance than we might ever imagine."

Malik went to his study and retrieved a military-issue canvas shoulder bag. "Here are the copies you made at Carlson's office." He withdrew some papers and a small magnifying glass. He handed them to Stone.

Stone took the scroll copies and laid them out on the kitchen table. She inspected them with the magnifying glass. "We need something more powerful than a magnifying glass," she said.

"Why are we wasting time looking at copies? Keller asked. "The real deal is underneath your fridge."

Malik nodded. " I am not ready to risk damage to the scroll until we get it to an appropriate facility designed to examine ancient texts."

Keller was watching Stone's every move. "Well, where would you suggest we go?'

Stone looked up. "We can't go back to Hebrew Union's lab. That's for sure. I never imagined Gadi Sagal or Professor Carlson could be thieves."

"I have a grad student at Tel Aviv University with access to the equipment we need." Malik yawned. "It has been a long day. I am starting to feel my age. Let's get a fresh start early in the morning, say 7:00 a.m.?"

Keller laughed. "That's two hours later than I usually get up professor, but that will work."

Malik went to his bedroom. Before he lay down, he placed his loaded Baretta beneath his pillow. He was taking no chances. Whoever bankrolled the Samaritans was not some-one to take for granted.

Hours later, the sound of heavy metal hitting the floor woke Malik with a start. He grabbed his gun and threw on a robe. Silently, he made his way down the hall to Keller and Stone's room. He placed his ear on the door. From the sounds within, either the Americans were wrestling with an intruder, or more likely, they were wrestling with each other. Either way, there was a lot of panting and groaning. He relaxed his grip on the gun, concluding that the earlier noise was Keller's weapon hitting the floor.

"Thank God no one got shot!" Malik thought with a chuckle. Lovemaking is such a life-affirming act, he mused, but for the rest of the night, he slept with the gun on his nightstand.

When the trio arrived in front of the Archeology Building at Tel Aviv University, a young man with a trim beard dressed in khakis and an open-collar blue shirt, approached with a broad smile and an outstretched hand.

"Abby and Aaron, permit me to introduce one of my students, Akiba Eltsur," Malik said, embracing their greeter. "He is an accomplished archeologist in his own right. In a few weeks, he will be defending his doctoral thesis. Then, like most newly minted PHD's, he will be unemployed."

"Thank you so much, Professor," Eltsur grinned, ushering them into the building and down to the basement.

"How come the lab is in the basement?" Keller asked, reading the sign over the steel doors at the far end of the corridor.

Eltsur replied, "For some in our country, archeology is the science of desecrating ancient cemeteries. Our Ultra-orthodox citizens frequently hold demonstrations in front of this building. It is a precaution. The equipment behind these doors is expensive. This department rarely gets a second chance at big-ticket items."

Malik sighed. "Israel is a *mish-mash* of many beliefs."

Eltsur swiped an ID card in front of an electronic lock and the light changed from red to green. He pulled open the door, switched on the lights, and invited his guests to enter.

The room was 10 meters by 10 meters. The subdued lighting revealed a variety of video monitors attached to machines. Most of the monitors were powered on, displaying screen-saver photos of various historical sites in Israel.

"Impressive," Stone said, surveying the equipment.

Eltsur sat down at a large console that straddled a corner of the counter opposite the doors. With a few keystrokes the system began booting up.

"May I have the document in question?" Eltsur asked.

Keller placed the towel-wrapped package on the end of the counter. He removed the cloth revealing the leather roll.

Eltsur reached for a small box on a shelf above the counter and extracted a pair of white cotton gloves. "The last thing I want to do is damage or contaminate your discovery." After putting the gloves on, he carefully untied the leather straps and began peeling away the cover. He then gently rolled open the scroll. He leaned down to get a closer look. "It is truly beautiful. The lettering is amazing." He looked up. "Where did you get this?"

Malik smiled, "If we tell you, we will have to kill you." He became serious. "If the bad guys learn you have read the document, they will kill you."

"You're kidding. Right, Professor?"

"Just get it under the scope, Akiba. And you must not tell anyone about our visit. For your safety and ours."

CHAPTER EIGHT

DATE: The Fifteenth Day of the Twelfth Month, In the Twenty-Fourth Year Since the Return of the Judean Exiles from Bavel [516 BCE]
TIME: First Hour of the Third Watch
PLACE: Jerusalem

The sudden sharp rocking of the prison cart on rough cobblestones signaled to Yeshai that he and his captors had arrived in Jerusalem. Two days had passed since his arrest. After the first day of the journey, heavy rains reduced their progress to a slow walk. As a result, he was very wet and very cold. A sudden jolt to the cart caused Yeshai to look up in time to see they were about to pass through a massive arched stone gate, flanked by sculpted lions. The lions protected the entry into Jerusalem from the North. Yeshai did not know what to expect on his arrival in the largest city in Judah. His grandfather Eli told him wondrous stories about Jerusalem in the days before its destruction and he had heard rumors from travelers in Samaria that the returnees from Bavel had made great progress in their restoration of the city. What little he could see through the bars of the prison cart appeared to confirm those rumors.

"This gate must be the end of the road leading from Jerusalem to Damascus," he thought. The craftsmanship evidenced by the gate made a statement about those now in charge of the city. Yeshai was filled with a sense of foreboding.

As the guards and cart completed their passage through the gate, Yeshai became aware, as if for the first time, of the masses of people around him. Most of them paid no attention to the prisoner in the cart. Others glanced briefly in his direction then turned away.

Yeshai listened to conversations going on around him. Most of these were in Aramaic, the language of the empire. A few were in Hebrew. "Did this mean that there were other Judeans from Samaria in Jerusalem?" he wondered. Since they appeared to be walking around freely, perhaps there was hope for him.

The cart came to a stop in a dark and narrow street and without a word to the dripping wet Yeshai, Calev pulled the prisoner to his feet. He then grabbed the *migbahat,* the now sponge-like priestly headdress lying next to him on the floor, and as an afterthought, threw it at him. Then he unlocked the shackles on Yeshai's wrists and feet.

With his hands now free, Yeshai placed the *migbahat* on his head.

Calev was filled with disgust. "You wear the headdress of a priest. Who did you steal it from?"

The question was followed by stinging blows to Yeshai's upper arms, first his right and then his left. Calev was not interested in anything Yeshai had to say.

Yeshai pleaded his case. "I stole it from no one. It is mine. I am the elected Head Priest of the Judeans in Samaria."

Calev had had enough. He knocked the *migbahat* from Yeshai's head. "You are a blasphemer and a traitor!"

Yeshai tried to remove any malice from the tone of his voice. "I am your kinsman from Judah. The only thing that separates you and me is the location of our exile—yours has been in Bavel, mine in Samaria."

Calev struck Yeshai again. "You arrogant piece of dung. You are no better than the ones the Bavlim left behind. You're all the same. You claim to be descendants of Judah, but you are all liars. I will never understand why we waste our time with questions and trials. You have violated the priestly purity of Judah by marrying the whores of Samaria. Your children's eyes testify to your rebellion against God."

Yeshai looked directly into Calev's eyes. "We are all one people dedicated to the one and only living God. Why are you doing this?"

Calev pushed Yeshai forward. "Join that line of prisoners against the wall over there."

Yeshai decided not to provoke his captor with another question.

A few moments later, Yeshai and the other prisoners, numbering about thirty, were ordered to walk down a narrow street between high stone walls. At the end of the street, they found themselves outside the walls of the city and in front of a makeshift prison compound made of wood.

Yeshai turned to look up at the substantial walls of the city they left behind. "Where are we, exactly?"

"We are below the Dung Gate," a fellow prisoner, looking as miserable and as wet as Yeshai, responded.

"Why do they call it that?"

"Anything thrown out of Jerusalem eventually ends up here--waste, garbage, dung, and Judeans from Samaria."

Before Yeshai could respond to the insult, he was segregated from his fellow prisoners and dragged by two burly Levite guards to a large, dark, goat-hair tent. The guards hoisted his hands above his head and tied them to a stout tent pole anchored deep into the dirt floor. His feet were bound together in front of him. He sat on the ground with his back against the pole. The canopy kept the steady rain from falling directly on his head but did not stop the rivulets of runoff from passing beneath his buttocks. He could not stop shivering, except when his pride got the better of him. He took in his new surroundings. Yeshai, son of Gilad, son of Eliezer, son of Achituv the priest, understood that the prisoner's comment was true. He had become part of the refuse dumped outside the city's gates.

Throughout the next day, at regular intervals, he was questioned by new pairs of guards. Whenever the interrogators would enter the tent, he would make a valiant effort to control his shivering. Anger gave him the inner strength to control his body. He was, after all, a *cohein,* a priest. They had no right or cause to treat him like a common criminal. Each time he asked, "Why are you doing this?" Yeshai never heard an answer, though, perhaps, it was contained in the blow that finally rendered him unconscious.

The sound of the downpour brought Yeshai back as the rain, driven by a strong West wind, began pouring into the makeshift prison. Was it minutes, hours, or days later? He had no way of knowing. As his head cleared, he could hear people entering the tent. Yeshai turned to face his next tormentors as two large guards dressed in identical dark brown tunics entered and took up positions at opposite ends of the large tent. Their torches cast shadows of dancing flames against the sidewalls. A third man, wearing a red wool over-tunic with black and white stripes at the edges and brandishing a dagger made of polished bronze, approached Yeshai. Yeshai held his breath and stared directly into the eyes of his murderer. If he was going to die, he was not going to close his eyes. The dagger passed the right side of Yeshai's face and began to cut the ropes binding him to the center pole. The ropes around his feet were severed next.

"Stand up!"

"Who are you?"

"I am Dov ben Asher, the captain of the High Priest's guard. You are my responsibility now. Make any effort to run or escape and you will be carved up on the spot," the dagger bearer warned. He was almost the same height as Yeshai but looked as if he weighed twice as much. He tossed a bundle made from coarse cloth and tied with thin string at Yeshai's feet.

"Put these on. Hurry, we don't have all night!"

Yeshai untied the bundle and found therewithin two garments, an undergarment with a drawstring and a simple un-dyed wool over-tunic. Worn leather sandals were at the bottom of the bundle. Both garments were loose fitting and very coarse, but they were dry and that was all that mattered to him.

"Follow me!" Ben Asher ordered.

"Where are you taking me?"

"Where you truly do not belong, Samaritan. Do not ask me any more questions. We haven't time." He spat out the word Samaritan as if he had eaten something foul and diseased.

An amazing sight greeted them when they exited the tent. The rain had stopped. The sky was free from clouds. The storm had passed and the stars, the host of heaven, were all in attendance. The Judean hills were coated in a thin film of ice. The nearly full moon cast more than enough light to make the ground appear to be pure silver. Had it not been so cold, they would have continued to stare at the incredible view.

Ben Asher pushed Yeshai forward on a narrow path. It might have been a true road before the destruction of Jerusalem. It was possible to make out the line where edging stones had once defined the roadway. Now most of the space was covered in debris and rubble. Fifty years before, the Bavlim had forced the left-behind Judean farmers to take apart the once great city walls, stone by stone, block by block. Judging by the size of the stones and blocks clogging the roadway, Yeshai concluded that they must be close to the location of the Sacred House. The presence of many Levites bearing torches and the level of activity surrounding them also seemed to confirm this observation.

Eli and Ben Asher arrived at a large pavilion defined by cloth stretched between posts that were each twelve cubits apart. "This is where I leave you. Go inside and wait for further instructions. Remember, you are still surrounded by Levites who would just as soon kill you as look at you. Do not try to escape."

An undulating goat's hair canopy, held aloft by thick poles four cubits high, created an impressive interior space. Yeshai estimated it was as large in area as the Samaritan Temple courtyard. The entire floor was covered in woven reed mats, each one a unique geometric design. At the opposite end of the pavilion was a raised platform covered in carpets. Cushions were placed on the platform for seating. Next to one of the cushions, on a wooden frame, Yeshai eyed a detailed drawing on a stretched sheet of parchment. He could not be certain, but he thought he might be looking at designs for the restoration of the Sacred House.

On the platform sat a heavily bearded priest dressed entirely in fine white linen, a blue linen *migbahat* on his head. Across his shoulders was a sky-blue robe made from a very unusual material that appeared to move like flowing water. The priest spoke Hebrew very carefully. "Come here that I may see your eyes. What is your name?"

"I am Yeshai, son of Gilad, son of Eliezer, son of Achituv from Gezer. I am the Head Priest of the Judeans in Samaria. Thank you for the dry clothes."

The priest muttered something in Aramaic, first to himself and then to Yeshai, "O-ho, 'head priest' so you say, so you say. Look at me!"

Yeshai stared at the tent wall behind the priest and said nothing.

The Judean on the platform rose to his feet. "I am Yeshuah ben Yo-tsadak, a direct descendant of the High Priest, Zadok, anointed to the service of the Holy One by the mighty King David."

Yeshai got down on his hands and knees and prostrated himself on the reed mat floor.

"At least you show decent manners for a Samaritan, I'll give you that."

"I am not a Samaritan! My grandfather, Eliezer, was an apprentice scribe in the Sacred House that stood in this place."

An enigmatic smile crossed the priest's face. "Actually, I know that. Get up! I also know that your grandfather and his brother, Zadok, rescued the sacred scrolls of our people from the hands of the Bavli. Do not look so surprised. We know all about you priests and scribes in Samaria. We also know that your grandmother was Shoshana bat Talmon, a Samaritan whore."

Yeshai lunged at the priest. From out of nowhere, two more Levite guards grabbed him from behind and pushed his face into the floor.

"Let him up!" Yeshua ben Yo-tsadak ordered.

Speaking into the floormat beneath his face, Yeshai growled. "My grandmother was but a child when your brother priest, Ezekiel ben Buzi, enlisted her as a messenger to the Samaritans. Without her, the sacred scrolls would have been destroyed by the Bavlim."

"Yes, yes, that is all well and good. We are well informed of the *drash* of Judeans living in Samaria."

Insulted by the priest's use of the word fable, he asked, "What do you mean, '*drash*'?"

The Judean priest turned Yeshai over onto his back with his foot so he could look into his eyes. "You know as well as I do that the Judeans who escaped exile by running to Samaria were all deserters. Your heroic tale was concocted by your grandparents to erase their shame. The Holy One who promised this land to our ancestors intended that the entire House of Judah would suffer exile. This was our punishment. Only through exile could we atone for our sins. You deserters have not suffered as we have suffered. Therefore, you have not participated in the atonement."

Two Levite guards lifted Yeshai to his feet. "As I look around this place, you, and your host of *cohanim* do not look as if you have suffered all that much. How is your own atonement progressing?"

"Your impudence will cost you, polluter of the seed of Aaron."

"Why am I here?" Yeshai shouted.

Yeshuah shifted on his cushion. He gazed about the pavilion and then ordered the Levite guards to leave. They protested, but he was insistent. They left the tent. He then lowered his voice, practically to a whisper. "Where are the Sacred Scrolls?"

"The Samaritan priests forced my *saba* to turn them over years ago."

"Do you think I am a fool? Our spies inform us that the Samaritans confiscated numerous copies of the sacred scrolls. The original Sacred Scrolls themselves remain hidden. Where are they?"

"You will still have to ask the Samaritans."

"Do not make me force this information from you."

"You cannot force from me what I do not know."

"You were their head priest. The scrolls were in your custody. The spies say that the stone hut in which the scrolls were preserved and guarded was empty by the time you were arrested. You must have hidden them elsewhere."

"How would I know where the Sacred Scrolls are? Do you now acknowledge the truth of what you so callously called a *drash*? Every Sacred Scroll copy was confiscated by the Samaritans.

"You are a liar! People will die because of your stubbornness."

Yeshuah ben Yo-tsadak arose from the platform and began walking back and forth in front of Yeshai, stroking his beard and reflecting on what he had just heard. "My spies tell me that you routinely offered sacrifices in the Samaritan polluted sham of a sacred house. If true, you have committed blasphemy against our Eternal God. Tell me where you have hidden the original Sacred Scrolls, and I will remove the charge of blasphemy from your list of crimes."

This much Yeshuah ben Yo-tsadak knew. The returnees from Bavel only carried with them copies of the Sacred Scrolls. Leaders of the Judeans in Bavel refused to allow the originals to make the journey to Jerusalem. Yeshua ben Yo-tsadak made it his personal mission to locate the Samaritan set of sacred scrolls and insure their safekeeping. Nevertheless, he could not fulfill this task. There was no secure way for him to send numbers of Judean soldiers north to Samaria. The political climate was tense, and the Samaritans would much prefer that all of the Judeans returned to Bavel. They did not like sharing the lands of Judah and Israel, now designated by the Persians as the Province Beyond the Rivers, with the returning exiles.

Yeshuah ben Yo-tsadak also knew that lately, marauding bands of Samaritan soldiers were killing Judeans from the south on sight. They were even so bold as to conduct night raids on Jerusalem, to disrupt the rebuilding of the Sacred House. If this so-called priest was to be believed, the Sacred Scrolls once preserved in Samaria were gone forever. But was he telling the truth?

"Set me free. I have done nothing wrong."

"Nothing wrong? Your own people have witnessed you worshipping in the sanctuary of the Samaritans and offering sacrifices there."

Yeshua ben Yo-tsadak wished to be done with the matter. He had better things to do than chase after scrolls that didn't exist. His path was now clear.

"You shall be made an example, burned at the stake for your crimes. Guards! Take this *mamzer* back to the tent of confinement. Bind him securely. Tomorrow, at sunrise, he will die for his insults to the God who redeemed us from exile."

Late into the night, Yeshai prayed for deliverance from his sentence. He turned over in his mind the actions his father and grandfather could have taken to keep the sacred scrolls safe. He was devastated by the realization that all of his potential solutions for them were no better than the course they ultimately followed. Yeshai was in a trap with no escape. He sought solace in his last hours of life by reciting the Psalms of King David. Just before dawn, he heard footsteps moving outside the tent. "I see now how You, O God, have chosen to answer my prayers. These Judeans from Bavel could not wait until the dawn. They have come to kill me now before anyone can offer a reprieve."

Suddenly the entrance flap parted, and a tall, dark skinned Persian officer dressed entirely in shimmering black robes entered the tent and immediately cut Yeshai's bonds with a silver dagger.

"Who are you?"

"I am Memukan, *Pecha* of Bavel and personal messenger of the emperor. We have no time to waste. Follow me!"

As they exited the tent, Yeshai caught sight of Levite Guards, motionless on the ground.

"Are they dead?"

"They will awaken when we are far away from here. If you don't want to die before sunrise, get moving!"

"Excellency, the Samaritan prisoner has escaped!" Dov ben Asher was not pleased to bring this news to the High Priest.

It was still dark outside the High Priest's pavilion. Yeshuah rubbed the sleep from his eyes. "How is this even possible?"

"Our men assigned to guard the prisoner were beaten unconscious. They cannot remember anything of the escape. "

"He must have had help."

"Who would dare to help a condemned Samaritan Jew?"

"The Persians, Excellency. I have questioned witnesses who awoke to the sound of horses leaving the prison compound. Based on their description of the size and outfitting of the horses, I believe that a Persian military unit of four or five soldiers freed the prisoner and provided him with his own mount. They set off in the direction of the Jericho road.

"But what would Persians want with the condemned?"

"I have no idea, your excellency, but it must be important enough to risk disturbing the delicate political balances of their empire."

"There is only one way to find out what this rescue means. We need to get them before they reach Jericho and the Persian military encampment there."

"Yes, Excellency."

"Well, get moving!"

"What shall we do if we catch up to them?"

"Bring them back to me in chains. I need to know what this rescue is all about. I intend to question them until I get answers."

"Are you not concerned this will bring us into an all-out war with Persia?"

"It is clear to me that the Judean priest from Samaria is of great value to the Persians. I need to know why."

CHAPTER NINE

DATE: March 18, 2009
TIME: 12:15 P.M. Local Time
PLACE: Archeology Building, Tel Aviv University

Akiba Eltsur took up a position in front of an expansive keyboard. He tapped a couple of keys, and an enormous LCD flat screen came to life on the wall.

Keller moved closer to the screen. "Now that I know what to look for, I have never seen so many *Taggim,* as you called them. They're all over the place."

Malik nodded. "Indeed. Sergeant Keller is absolutely correct. We can now confirm that there are no more than twenty-two points."

Akiba turned to face Malik. "It's a letter substitution code, Professor."

"We already concluded that, Akiba. Now we need to view the scroll, one letter at a time, so we can list the letters revealed by the coded message, in order. It's not a sophisticated cipher, but it would have been very effective if it was simply passed off as a decorated scroll and nothing more."

For the next hour and a half, Akiba patiently moved from letter to letter as Malik and Stone counted the points and converted them into Hebrew letters.

Keller contented himself with watching the others work to reveal the message. "Why are you not putting spaces between the words, Abby...uh Lieutenant?" He asked.

"Because Hebrew, at the time this scroll was written, did not put spaces between words. We want to see the letters without making assumptions about what words they form."

"So, what does it all mean?" Keller asked.

"*Savlanut*! Sergeant, *Savlanut!* Be patient and we shall have our answer."

"I'm already having trouble with making out the first word," Stone said.

"What word begins with the letters *samech hey kuph*? I believe the second word is *bateivah*...'in a box,' or 'in the box.'"

Eltsur nodded, "Rabbi, I agree with your translation of the second word. But I am also having trouble with these first three letters. They don't make sense."

Malik looked at the letters. "They don't make sense because they might be the first example in history of an abbreviation in the Hebrew language. *Samech, hey, kuph... sefer hakodesh*. What do you think?"

"Brilliant!" Stone exclaimed.

"How about letting a dumb Marine in on this?" Keller asked.

Stone smiled. "It's not **a** word. Sergeant. It is possibly two words. *Sefer hakodesh*, it *means*, 'The Sacred Scroll.'"

"Isn't this the sacred scroll? Is there another?"

"Sergeant, this is not a sacred scroll. It is a Biblical psalm. At this point we can't be sure of anything. Let's just see where this text is leading us." Malik said.

Two more hours of painstaking analysis produced a series of words, but it was not altogether clear what their meaning was. Eltsur wrote an English translation below the Hebrew:

THE SACRED SCROLL IS IN THE BOX BENEATH SHOSHANA BAT TALMON, WIFE OF ELIEZER BEN ACHI-TUV, IN THE SACRED CAVE NEXT TO MT GERIZIM.

D/E/H/S.

Eltsur walked closer to the white board with the list of Hebrew words. "What do you think *dalet aleph hey samech* means?"

Stone stared at the letters and shook her head in frustration. "I have no idea. But I do believe that coming at the end of the message those letters might be intended to reveal the scroll code author's identity."

Eltsur's head nodded. "You mean like a signature?"

"That could be anyone!" Keller said. "Do you remember when we were in the tea shop you got all excited thinking that the scroll was what you called, 'The Ezra Scroll'. Maybe someone named Ezra wrote and signed it."

Malik closed his eyes for a moment. "*Divrei Ezra HaSofer,* that might be it.""

Eltsur's eyes were wide in amazement. "Wait a minute! "You're not saying that this scroll was written by the Biblical Ezra himself? Are you? You are! *Oi vavoi!*"

Malik placed a hand on Eltsur's shoulders. "Calm down, Akiba. This is just one hypothesis. We will have to test others. There is no time to lose. Remember, there are people who may want to stop us from getting answers."

Keller's hand moved to his concealed gun.

Malik paced back and forth while he studied the decoded message that confronted him from the whiteboard. "Rabbi, just give me your best guess so far."

Stone surveyed her notes on a legal pad. "I do not know who these named people are. I am stuck on the phrase "sacred cave." What is a sacred cave and where would it be located?"

Keller stood next to Stone. "How many caves are mentioned in the Bible? Are any of them sacred? The only cave in the Bible I know about is the Cave of the Patriarchs. Is that a sacred cave?"

"You did it, Sergeant! Of course! That's it! A sacred cave would be a burial site. That is how bodies were disposed of in ancient Israel. We are being directed to a burial cave."

Malik's brows rose in surprise. "Really, are you sure?"

Keller was feeling confident about his contribution to the discussion. "Ancient Israelite custom was to locate a natural cave or carve one out of limestone or sandstone and use it for the final resting place of human remains."

Stone looked at Keller in wonder. "Sergeant, you never cease to surprise me. Just when I assume that you have been raised with the barest minimum of a Jewish education, you demonstrate that you must have been listening a few times in Hebrew School."

"Well Lieutenant Stone, the story of the death of Sarah was my Bar Mitzvah Torah portion. Genesis: Chapter Twenty-three. Abraham purchases the cave at Machpelah to bury his wife. Didn't they dig a hole in the floor of the cave and just bury her there?"

Stone cracked a thin smile. "It wasn't that simple. They would carve shelves or niches into the walls and lay the bodies on the shelves, wrapped in linen shrouds. The bodies would be allowed to decay naturally, and then family members would return to the cave and gather the bones of the deceased and place them in clay or stone boxes. Archeologists use the Latin term 'ossuaries'. In modern Hebrew they are called 'gloskamot.' This code calls it simply 'a box.' The boxes would have the names of the deceased inscribed on one side. The boxes would then be placed on a shelf, probably an upper shelf."

So, Rabbi, you think that we are being directed to a burial cave near Mt Gerizim?" Malik asked.

Stone furrowed her brow. "That is what it feels like, but it does not make historical sense."

Keller was lost. "What is that supposed to mean?"

"There were no Judeans in Samaria at that time," said Stone.

"I know you're a Lieutenant and rabbi and all, but what makes you so sure?"

"Well, Sergeant, please forgive me but I cannot answer your question without entering full teaching mode. Think you can handle a deep dive into the text of the *TANACH*?"

Keller moved his hands in a gathering motion. "Bring it on!"

"All of the Biblical evidence suggests that there was no love lost between Judeans and Samaritans."

"Isn't that a curious turn of phrase?" Malik asked.

Stone nodded in agreement. "Actually, I believe there **was** love lost between the Samaritans and the Judeans. I believe that their relationship began as one between student and teacher. The Samaritans were the students, the Judeans were their teachers in learning how to worship the god of Israel."

"There is a foolproof way to settle this question," Akiba said.

"What's that?"

"Find the burial cave of Shoshana bat Talmon."

CHAPTER TEN

DATE: The Sixteenth Day of the Twelfth Month, In the Twenty-Fourth Year Since the Return of the Judean Exiles from Bavel [516 BCE]
TIME: Third Hour of the First Watch
PLACE: The Road to Jericho

Yeshai and his rescuers made their escape from Jerusalem on five magnificent Persian horses, each the color of the night sky. They rode in complete silence toward the sunrise for an hour. When rays of light crept over the eastern horizon, the man called Memukan ordered two of his escorts to double back and scout the road behind them. "We will wait for you here. If the road behind us is clear, we shall proceed. I want to make sure that our departure from Jerusalem went unnoticed." Then Memukan dismounted and gave the order to water and rest the remaining horses.

A winter stream running parallel to the road had captured water from the rain of the previous day. Everyone including the horses drank their fill. The water was clear and cool. For Yeshai, it was time to get some answers. He cleared his throat and began haltingly in Aramaic, the language of the Empire. "Who sent you and why are you doing this? Am I your prisoner?"

"You have an important friend in Bavel. I should say, in Pumbedita, to be more exact. The truth is he is not just a friend; he is your cousin. His name is Hilkiah ben Shallum ben Zadok. He made me swear an oath to bring you to him. He is very concerned about the Sacred Scrolls in your care, the twelve rescued by your grandfather, Eli. For the past month, we have been riding all over Samaria and Judah looking for you. You were not easy to locate."

"Now you? Am I only worthy of rescue because of the scrolls? Well, I have some difficult news for you. The scrolls have not been in the possession of my family or me for quite some time. That is why the Judean High Priest, Yehoshua ben Yo-tsadak, wanted to kill me. I gave him the same news. You might as well kill me and get it over with."

At that moment, the two soldiers sent to scout out the road behind the Persians returned. "Excellency, the Judeans are pursuing us and are only a half hour's ride away!"

"I do not want a fight with them. If we engage, the secret purpose of our mission will be compromised. Mount up everyone! We need to get moving."

Struggling to harness his horse, Yeshai shouted at Memukan over the noise of the soldiers making ready to leave. "What secret mission?"

Settling into his own saddle, Memukan resumed his conversation with Yeshai, while keeping a close watch on his soldiers. "We are not here to kill you. There are two parts to our mission: first, find the scrolls and second, bring you to Pumbedita."

"I still do not understand."

The Pecha signaled his riders to move out. He maneuvered his horse next to Yeshai. "A disaster has befallen your family. Your cousin Hilkiah is dying. When he realized that he did not have long to live, he became desperate to locate you and bring you to him. If his enemies knew I was going to bring you to Bavel, they would seek to kill me and you."

Yeshai stared at Memukan. "Does his family know about this? Do they know I am coming to them?"

"Don't be a fool. How could they know you are coming if, until a day ago, I had no idea where to find you? The secrecy he demanded was to protect his loved ones. He insisted that no one in his family be told of this mission, not his wife nor his father-in-law. Your place now is in Bavel. By the time we return, Hilkiah may already be dead, and that would make you last of the Ben Achituv scribes."

"The priests returned from exile in Bavel were about to have me burned at the stake. Why would I want to journey all the way to Bavel and place myself under the rule of their brothers?"

"Perhaps to remove the sentence of death which hangs over you. I carry the Emperor's seal."

"Am I supposed to be impressed?"

Memukan shook his head. "The Emperor's Median priests have prophesied that Judah must be restored before the throne of Persia will be secure."

"What does that have to do with Judean scribes?"

"In the days of Cyrus, your great aunt Miryam, wife of Zadok ben Achituv, created scribal schools among the Judeans in Bavel. The Emperor was greatly impressed with her skill and dedication. He asked her to read to him from the scrolls. Over the course of several days, she read to His Majesty from the scrolls of your people."

"I still do not see what the traditions of my people have to do with the exalted Emperor of Persia."

"The Emperor developed great respect for your God. He believed that his victories over the Bavlim were because of the power of the God of Judah. He inquired of Miryam as to what steps he should take to secure his throne. She saw this as a moment of great opportunity, so she responded that the Emperor must protect the Judeans and their sacred scrolls. You are needed in Bavel to continue copying, protecting, and preserving those scrolls and the scribal schools as well."

Memukan ordered his soldiers to pick up the pace, though he maintained a calmness in his voice.

Yeshai was not to be deterred. "Surely my Bavli cousins have trained many capable scribes, just as my family did in Samaria."

"That may be so, but in the shadow of the illness that has befallen Hilkiah, your scribes in Bavel have divided into factions. Some wish to continue their life in Bavel; others insist that the only place for Judeans is in Judah."

"But that is a dispute for Judeans, not Persians."

"It is not so simple. Have you not heard of the many gifts the empire has bestowed upon the Judeans for the building of their Sacred House and their nation? Do you think those gifts come without a price? The return of the Judeans from exile was not just a sign of Cyrus's respect for your God. He expected Judean loyalty in return. You were expected to guard the empire against the grand ambitions of the Egyptians. Only a united Judean people can hope to stand against the mighty pharaohs. "

"They cannot even stand up to the might of Samaria; how are they supposed to stand up to Egypt?"

"Our enemies wish to encourage divisions among the nations of the empire, to weaken the power of the sons of Cyrus. Your cousin Hilkiah saw great danger."

"I never even met him!"

"You will enjoy his wisdom. He studies the workings of our empire much as he studies your Sacred Scrolls, with great intensity."

"With what result?"

"He now worries that if Egypt defeats Persia and expels her garrisons from the region, the Judeans would be blamed. He also believes that only one such as you, trained in the Sacred Scrolls, could bring the factions back together. You are living proof that all of the scrolls are the heritage of Judah. Your God intended for them to be symbols of national unity. He believes that because you lived in Samaria, you were unpolluted by the subservient stench of exile."

"Why is it you and not some Judean who was sent to find me?"

"I have known Hilkiah since he was a child. I am his friend." Memukan reached into a leather pouch attached to his saddle. "Here is my seal from the Emperor as well as Hilkiah's own seal. I hope he is still alive when we return."

Yeshai rubbed Hilkiah's cylinder seal between his thumb and first finger. Then he looked carefully at the carved impression. The seal revealed its owner's identity—*Hilkiah ben Shallum ben Zadok ben Achituv M'gezer*. But it was the phrase which followed Hilkiah's name that took Yeshai's breath away--*Shomer Sefer Torat Moshe*, "Guardian of the scroll of the teaching of Moses."

Yeshai's mind was made up. "I will continue on with you on one condition."

"Priest, you are in no position to make demands!"

"I will go with you, but first we must turn around and head north to the village of Anatoth."

"You will place yourself in the territory of the very people who would have you roasted on a stake. You said so yourself."

"Listen to me," Yeshai said. "Your own soldiers have told you that the Judeans are pursuing us! If we can cover our tracks as we head north, we can lose them. They will be expecting us to head for Jericho. This detour will help us."

"What is so special about Anatoth?" Memukan asked.

"There is a sacred scroll there."

"You said the Sacred Scrolls are in the hands of the Samaritans."

"Yes, the twelve Sacred Scrolls are no longer in my family's possession. But there is another a sacred scroll still hidden in Samaria. The contents of the twelve other scrolls are contained within that single scroll. My grandfather, Eli, made a copy of that scroll. The original he returned to its hiding place. It is secure. *Saba* gave the only other copy to the priests of Anatoth for safe keeping."

"Just like that he gave it to other priests?" Memukan was having difficulty believing Yeshai's tale.

"The priests of Anatoth are trustworthy. They never sank into the idol worship of the Jerusalem priests. Eli knew that they would not hand the scroll over to the Jerusalem priests. There has been enmity between Anatoth and Jerusalem since the days of the prophet Jeremiah."

"Who?"

"Never mind. Will you take me to Anatoth?

"Take these." Memukan reached into another saddlebag on his mount. He handed Yeshai a short bronze dagger and a bronze curved sword. "We may have to fight our way out of Anatoth. I hope this scroll is worth it."

"Indeed, it is the word of our God through Moses his prophet."

"So be it. Then we have no other choice but to keep riding. After we turn away from the Jericho Road and start heading to Anatoth, we can look for a watering and grazing area for the horses. When we do stop for a rest, there is one other thing you must do."

"And what is that?"

"Shave your head. It is the only way to ensure that the Jerusalem based Judean priests will ignore you. By now they will have informants everywhere looking for you."

"I am a Nazirite."

"What does that mean?"

"It means I have sworn an oath before the God of my ancestors. I made a promise to Him."

"Why would you do that?"

Why indeed? Yeshai thought. "I wanted my wife and son to live."

Memukan turned his head toward Yeshai and looked him directly in the eyes. He saw tears flowing down his road-dusted cheeks. Yeshai continued to speak, but his tone was lifeless and flat.

"When a Judean seeks the help of the Almighty for a personal reason, he takes a Nazirite oath. He gives up all manner of strong drink and is not allowed to cut his hair. Other Judeans, when they see such a person, know immediately that he has taken the Nazirite oath. In most cases they show him great respect."

"Did your god respect your oath? Did your wife and son live?" Memukan asked.

"No," Yeshai whispered.

"I do not know all of your Judean customs, but where I come from, if the gods do not do as you have begged them to do, you are released from your oath. When did they die?"

"Three years, seven months, and fourteen days ago." The words lodged in Yeshai's throat as if he was swallowing a stick from a thorn bush.

"Is this sacred scroll you seek important to your god?" Memukan asked.

"I believe it is. Yes."

"Do you also believe that your god wants you to carry it to your family in Bavel?"

"I do."

"So, until you deliver the scroll, your god wants you alive, correct?"

Yeshai nodded.

"The only way you are going to arrive in Bavel alive is if you disguise yourself as one of my people."

The Persians turned away from the Jericho Road around the time that the sun reached its highest elevation overhead. The riders dismounted and walked their horses to yet another wadi filled with rushing rainwater from the previous day's storm. Memukan handed Yeshai two knives. The first had a polished olive wood handle. It was a straight flint blade half a handbreadth long. This was for cutting the hair close to the head before shaving. The second knife was a small, curved flint knife with an extremely sharp edge. This was for the actual shaving of the head.

Yeshai was surprised at how well the knives worked. Memukan advised him to wet his hair completely. This made shaving easier and less painful. In less than an hour, his head was mostly smooth and slick, except for the cuts above the back of his neck.

Memukan looked Yeshai over carefully, slowly walking a circle around him. "Not bad for a Judean. You must have some Persian blood in you. Here, put these on." Memukan handed Yeshai a black cotton tunic and a heavy leather Persian breastplate and back piece.

When Memukan and his soldiers arrived in Anatoth three hours later, Yeshai looked as if he had been in the Emperor's service his entire life. Memukan barked a few words in Persian and the real Persian soldiers dismounted. Yeshai did as well. They walked single file, leading their horses to the water trough in the center of the village. They secured the horses to metal rings attached to the trough.

A small group of villagers, all dressed as *cohanim,* slowly approached the five Persians and bowed toward them with hands opened and outstretched, in a gesture of cautious welcome. They addressed the Persians in Aramaic. "My lords, welcome to Anatoth! How might we be able to serve you?"

Yeshai stepped in front of Memukan and his soldiers and announced his presence in Hebrew. *"Ani Yeshai ben Gilad ben Eli, Hasofer mishomron.* I am Yeshai, son of Gilad, son of Eli the scribe from Samaria. I have come to retrieve the scroll my grandfather left in your care."

The Jaws of the priests of Anatoth dropped open in astonishment when they realized that a Persian soldier was speaking to them in flawless Hebrew. "Do all of the soldiers of the Empire study our language? No wonder your people rule the world."

Yeshai continued his attempt to engage with the priests. "It's me, Yeshai ben Gilad, your brother priest!"

The priests of Anatoth shook their heads in disgust and disbelief. Their cautious courtesy disappeared. "No brother of ours would be caught dead with a shaved head wearing images of Persian gods on leather battle dress. You may speak our tongue, but you are no priest of Judah."

Memukan stepped in front of Yeshai to prevent him from being attacked. He drew his sword and gestured towards the priests that they should move back. The other Persians drew their swords and formed a defensive line in front of Yeshai and Memukan.

"You need to hear this man's story. He is telling the truth. He had to adopt this disguise to save his life. I know him to be a faithful Judean priest, leader of the Judean exiles in Samaria. Hear him out!"

The confrontation with the priests of Anatoth had drawn a crowd. Now, men women and children of the village stared at the bald Persian who claimed to be the head Judean priest of Samaria.

Yeshai told his story, just as he recounted it for Memukan on their journey to Anatoth. At the end of his narrative, heads nodded in understanding. The villagers' commitment to welcoming and caring for sojourners overcame their unease with Yeshai's un-Judean appearance. But no one yet said a word about the reason for their visit, retrieving the scroll Eli entrusted to them.

The wayfarers were invited to bathe and refresh themselves. A simple meal was prepared for them and served in a large communal dining room. It seemed as though the entire village was present. As they were eating, Yeshai noted several small meetings taking place among the elders of the village. One of the Persian soldiers asked Yeshai if he knew what was going on. "I think they are trying to decide whether to turn the scroll over to me or not."

"They had better make up their minds because we are leaving this place at sunrise, Pecha's orders."

"Not unless I have the scroll."

The issue was not decided. They spent the night in the home of the chief priest of the village. Yeshai could not sleep. He worried about what he would do if he had to leave the scroll behind. When dawn arose, Yeshai walked outside of the home and recited morning prayers, as he had done all his life. Then, with an overwhelming sense of failure, he joined the Persians in packing their few belongings, filling their waterskins, and readying the horses for departure.

"You cannot leave without this," said the chief priest of the village, as he handed a scroll to Yeshai. He knew at once that this was the scroll written by Eliezer ben Achituv. The wax seal binding the scroll was not broken. No one had read or copied the scroll. Tears streamed down his face as he embraced the priest with thanks.

"May I ask a question?"

"Of course you may."

"What finally made you decide to give the scroll to me?"

"I made the decision when my daughter reported seeing you saying your morning prayers. Then I knew you were who you claimed to be." The chief priest then pressed a small scroll into Yeshai's hands. "Take this with you to the Judeans still in exile."

"What is it?"

"These are the words of prophecy pronounced by our brother, Yeremiyahu, in the days of the last kings of Judah. The God of our ancestors revealed to Yeremiyahu what would befall Jerusalem and Judah. Perhaps this scroll and its message will help our brothers in Bavel remain faithful to the Creator of the world. I fear that the priests now in control of rebuilding Jerusalem are failing. They are becoming lazy in their service to our God. There will be more disasters to follow. May the God of our ancestors keep you safe on your journey."

Before Yeshai could question the priest further about the scroll or his concerns for the rebuilding of Jerusalem, Memukan ordered the party forward on the road out of Anatoth.

"Am I worthy to bear so much responsibility?" Yeshai wondered.

CHAPTER ELEVEN

DATE: March 18, 2009
TIME: 12:50 P.M. Local Time
PLACE: Archeology Building, Tel Aviv University

"Why would Samaritans need Judean priests to teach them about God? Didn't they have their own gods?"

Akiba laughed. "In those days, Aaron, all gods were local. The people dragged into exile by the Assyrians from somewhere in the east, were abandoned in the territory of Shomron. For these exiles, being cut off from their homeland meant that they were also cut off from their gods. They believed that their gods could not protect them in the hills of Samaria. The leaders of those exiles from the east sought a way to connect with the local gods, who, as luck would have it, happened to be the one god of Israel.

Stone continued. "An account in the Hebrew Bible confirms this story. The Second Book of Kings records that sometime after 721 BCE, the Assyrians conquered the Northern Kingdom of Israel. Following their usual practice in time of war, the Assyrians removed and exiled the local Israelites, the Ten Tribes of Israel, and brought in replacement peoples. Because the replacements ultimately settled in Samaria, we now call them and their descendants Samaritans.

"Upon their arrival they made a request of the Assyrian king. They asked for an exiled Israelite priest to be returned to Samaria so that he would teach them about the god of the territory. But I have never been convinced that is what happened."

Malik stroked his chin for a moment. "OK, what do you think happened then?"

"I believe the new arrivals invited Judeans, not Israelites, to Samaria to teach them," Stone said. "They sought out Judean priests because they were seen as being favored by their god."

"You know, for a rabbi, you're very smart."

Stone rolled her eyes and glared at Malik. "I try."

Eltsur spoke up. "Professor, isn't it your theory that when the Temple of Solomon was destroyed, not all of the Judean leadership went into exile in Babylonia? If that was the case, why would the Book of Kings say specifically it was an exiled Israelite priest that was returned to Samaria?"

Malik began to rock back and forth from his heels to his toes. "Perhaps the tradition of the Samaritans requesting a Judean priest was intentionally altered by the Judean editors of those texts to read 'Israelite priest,' in order to discredit the Samaritans," Malik said.

"Why would they do that?" Keller asked.

"Maybe, after a couple of centuries, the Samaritans became a threat to the Judeans. A major piece of Judean theology expressed in the *TANACH* was that the population of the Northern Kingdom of Israel was exiled because of their rampant idolatry. If the priestly tutor to the Samaritans was from the Kingdom of Israel, his faithfulness to the God of Abraham would have been suspect. As a result, the Samaritans' understanding of God would have been seen as flawed. I just think the Judeans were uncomfortable with the truth, that one of their own priests instructed the Samaritans."

Eltsur pointed to the enlarged image of the scroll on the screen. "Now, it could be that your theory has support from the evidence."

Malik shook his head in disagreement. "The Ezra scroll is not evidence...yet. It is my conviction that many Judeans escaped the annihilation of Jerusalem, slavery, and exile, by fleeing north into Samaria. If there was already a small contingent of Judean *cohanim*—priests—living among the Samaritans, they might have persuaded their hosts to allow the new refugees join them."

"How did you ever come up with this idea?" Keller asked.

"Do you recall my conversation with you about memorizing the genealogy of my family?"

"It's the last thing I remember before the bomb went off outside the tea shop."

"The first three names on that list are Achituv, Zadok ben Achituv, and Eliezer ben Achituv *m'shomron*. All of them were from a priestly clan, but Eliezer is the only one known as 'from Samaria'. My family tradition says he settled in Samaria. Eliezer, 'Eli,' as we affectionately refer to him, is the brother of Zadok. Zadok ben Achituv went into exile in Babylonia."

"How do you know that?"

"Because, Sergeant, I am descended from Ezra, and Ezra is descended from Zadok. His—my—genealogy is all there in the book of Ezra."

"Let me see if I am getting all of this." Stone began to outline a sequence of events on a clean section of the whiteboard. "You are saying that:

1. In 586 BCE, when the Babylonians took Jerusalem, some Judeans went into hiding or exile in Samaria.

2. While waiting for their exile to end, one or more of the Judeans hid something valuable in Samaria.

3. More than a century later, around 445 BCE, Ezra knew where this object was hidden, and he wrote a coded text describing the location of the object.

4. The location of the object is a bone box in a burial cave in Samaria."

Stone put the marker down. "Does that about sum it up?"

"Essentially."

"OK, Professor, what do you think this hidden object is?" Eltsur asked.

"An original Torah."

"You mean an early copy of the Torah?"

"No, I mean an original Torah. There is a great deal of circumstantial evidence that points to Ezra as the actual editor of the original Torah, the Torah we read from on Shabbat and the Festivals. While there were many sacred traditions and stories written before the time of Ezra, no coherent Torah with a national story and theology existed. I believe that the Ezra scroll is telling us where this original Torah may be found."

"Wow!"

"Wow, indeed!"

"Wait a minute! Your theory cannot be right. If the original Torah is hidden in a bone box in Samaria, Ezra could not have brought it back from the Babylonian exile," Keller said.

Malik nodded. "When you are right, Sergeant, you are right."

"What if there were two Torahs?" Stone asked. "What if the Samaritan-based Judean exiles wrote their own Torah or what if they had written the first Torah and then shared it with the Judean exiles in Babylonia?"

"Why does Ezra want anyone to know the location of the first Torah?" Eltsur asked.

"Maybe it was his way of giving authenticity to his own Torah," Stone said. "It's like he's saying my Torah is just a copy of the original, which is hidden in Samaria."

"This is getting way too complicated. We need to operate on what we actually know," Malik said.

"There may be issues we can never resolve," Stone said. "Just for the sake of argument, let us suppose that one or more Judeans living in Samaria invents a Torah."

"Invents?"

"Exactly. Using existing materials, stories, legends, traditions, and things made up on the spot, he/she/they put together a theological history of the house of Israel." Stone smiled broadly as she warmed up to her hypothesis. "Let's further assume the inventor is proud of his work," she continued. "He sends a copy to someone he trusts. Eventually, perhaps over the course of fifty or ninety years, the Torah finds its way into the possession of Ezra, the priest and scribe--and Professor Malik's grandfather fifty generations removed. At some point, Ezra realizes that the Torah might be a valuable asset in his battle to unify the Judeans and restore the descendants of Israel to their former glory. He edits, writes, invents his own version. Maybe it's the same. Maybe it's different. He presents it to the people as the scroll of the Teaching of Moses."

"And they buy it? Just like that?" Keller asked.

"Sergeant, if you read the beginning of the Book of Nehemiah, it paints a bleak picture of Judean life, nearly ninety years after the exile was ended," Malik explained. "Every nation needs its founding myth. George Washington never lied. In a time of desperation, people cling to hope and pride. The Torah would give them the sense that, indeed, their exile is over, and that they have a sacred purpose."

Keller remained unconvinced. "I still don't understand why Ezra wanted to inform someone about the existence of the first Torah."

"Get him on the phone and ask him," Malik said.

"It's a fair question," Keller said.

Malik nodded. "I'm just agreeing with Rabbi Stone. There are some issues we may never resolve. Our next task is to try to locate the Samaritan bone box."

"Good luck with that one," said Eltsur.

Keller was skeptical. "So, does that mean we should we be going to Mt. Gerizim? By the way, where is that?"

Eltsur bent over, reached into his backpack on the floor and produced a road map of Israel. He unfolded it and placed it on the counter. He picked up a pen a drew a circle on the map. "There, on the West Bank, near Nablus."

Keller smirked. "Are you afraid of getting lost? Do you always carry a map around with you?"

"It's an archeologist thing. I even carry a trowel and a small paint brush in case I need to do an impromptu excavation."

"Well, I have a feeling that the Palestinian Authority is not going to allow a bunch of Jews to go rooting around the hillsides, looking for a burial cave."

Stone stared in silence at the white board. "We need to know more about the traditions surrounding the use of bone boxes. Can you get me into the research areas of the Israel Museum, Professor? My sense is that the Museum is not going to be any more receptive to us looking for original Torahs than the Palestinian Authority would be."

Malik nodded. "You are probably more right than you realize. They do not routinely extend professional courtesies to outsiders like us," he said as he reached for his cell phone.

Stone, Keller, and Eltsur continued to stare at the message on the white board.

Keller spoke first. "Are you sure we have this correct? Is this the only explanation?"

Stone turned to him. "It is the one that makes the most sense, given the circumstances of the scroll's discovery. We need to follow this lead until it becomes a dead end, but I really think we are on the right track."

Malik was closing his flip phone as he returned to them. "I called in a couple of favors. We need to get to Jerusalem before the museum closes."

At that moment, the first two musical phrases of *Hatikvah* sounded in the basement lab. It was Malik's ring tone. The flip phone was still in his hand. He opened it, listened for a brief moment, then closed the phone.

"Sergeant, secure the scroll," Malik said, his tone rushed. "Akibah, we cannot thank you enough for your assistance in this matter. Thank you for the use of the University's equipment." Then he turned to Stone and Keller. "We must postpone our visit to the museum. We have been summoned to the Tel Aviv District Police Headquarters. Lavi says he has some important information he needs to impart to us."

PART II: A FAMILY REUNION

When brothers live together and one of them dies without a son, his widow shall not be married to a stranger outside the family. Her husband's brother shall come to her and take her in marriage, fulfilling the duty of a brother-in-law. The firstborn son she bears will perpetuate the name of the dead brother, so that his name will not be erased from Israel. (Deuteronomy 25:5-6)

CHAPTER TWELVE

DATE: Twentieth day of the First Month, in the Seventy-first Year Since the Destruction of Jerusalem. [515 BCE]
TIME: In the second hour of the first watch.
LOCATION: The Landing on the River Frat, Pumbedita

One month and four days had passed since Memukan, Yeshai, and Memukan's soldiers departed from Anatoth in Judah. On their journey they avoided contact with local populations whenever possible. Their vigilance protected them as much as did their prayers. There was no sign of their Judean pursuers.

Yeshai and the Persians had spent the last two weeks of their journey on a *kalak,* a large river raft made of timber and supported by inflated animal skins, and now the time had come for him to face his cousins. He looked out at the riverbank from the center of the deck and, as veteran crew member worked the rudder to line the vessel up parallel to the landing, Yeshai wondered how he, his head still clean shaven, would be received among the Judean exiles still in Bavel. The ship's Bavli master shouted commands to the remaining crew to prepare to secure the vessel once it made contact with the shore, but Yeshai was more focused on the view, one unlike anything he had ever seen in Samaria or Judah. He could feel the energy of the bustling waterfront. Woven reed canopies built on stilts were at least four cubits above the ground. They sheltered clay jars, large straw baskets, and wooden boxes that contained a dizzying variety of goods.

Memukan placed his hand on Yeshai's shoulder as he was about to disembark. "It will take some time to unload our horses and gear. Wait for us at the gate to the city. Do not enter on your own."

Yeshai stared at the activity on the landing. "I just want to stretch my legs. I will do as you have ordered."

Yeshai approached a wide street that appeared to be headed in the direction of the walled city. He estimated that it would take half an hour to walk the distance from the riverfront to the walls. Yeshai learned from a local resident who was a passenger on the raft that the town had suffered a devastating flood some years before and was so completely destroyed that the local notables decided to rebuild the city on much higher ground. Tall grasses and reeds growing in abundance were confirmation that this part of Pumbedita was indeed a flood zone.

The main city was surrounded by walls of reddish-brown mud brick that went on for a great distance in both directions away from the entrance to the city. Beautifully carved sandstone lions stood as sentinels atop the towers that formed the gate.

Memukan and his soldiers caught up with Yeshai outside the city gate. They were leading his horse. Yeshai mounted and looked to Memukan for some assurance that his Persian disguise was still capable of fooling the locals. Memukan said nothing and rode on at the head of the small party.

Yeshai was captivated by the unfamiliar sights and sounds as he passed through the gate and entered the largest city he had ever seen. The lushness and wealth on display in Pumbedita was impressive. The color of the structures was the same as that of the ground beneath their feet. Bright colors could be glimpsed from clothing or cloth suspended on ropes behind each house, drying in the soft breeze from the East. Each home had its own vegetable garden in front and a small stable in the back. Yeshai was surprised at the number of Judeans present at every turn. He recognized them because they dressed in a similar manner to their brothers and sisters in Judah. There were differences, however, in small bits and pieces of gold and silver jewelry many wore on open but modest display. The palpable social and political tensions of the Land of Israel were absent here. It was a wonder to Yeshai to ride among a people who were not afraid, not even of Persian soldiers.

"Son of Gilad, our journey together ends here," Memukan announced with no hint of concern. The group halted at the head of a street that led away from a small open square. There was nothing particularly distinguishing about the street or the square, which made Yeshai curious as to why Memukan chose to stop in this particular place.

Memukan pointed. *"Yahud*, your family lives on this street."

"Should you not introduce me to them?"

"Your scribal skills and your knowledge of your family will earn you their acceptance. Besides, you bear a strong resemblance to your cousin. Go now! It is the fourth house ahead, on your left. May the god who protected you on your journey keep you all the days of your life."

"May He do so also for you. How may I adequately thank you for saving my life?"

"You may not. It is the Emperor you must thank." And with that, Memukan and his soldiers wheeled and rode away from the square.

Yeshai dismounted and led his horse toward the home of his cousin, Hilkiah. It was identical in size and shape to the other houses on the narrow street. Upright pillars connected by a stone arch marked the entrance, but there was no gate. The hinges where once a gate might have been attached were red with rust. Yeshai tethered his horse to one of the pillars. It was difficult for Yeshai to imagine a place where gates were not required for protection from bandits.

A short stone path led to the front door. A small niche about the size of a human finger was hollowed out of the right side of the doorpost. A delicate, fired-clay filigree concealed the presence of a tiny scroll. The simple *mezuzah* on the doorpost silently announced that this was the home of a Judean who still maintained the traditions of his ancestors. Yeshai let his fingers linger on the small scroll container, then slowly and deliberately brought them to his lips. In a silent prayer he thanked the God of his ancestors for seeing him safely to the home of his family in Bavel. At least he hoped it was the home of his family. Before he could announce his presence, the heavy door with wrought iron hinges opened before him.

"My lord, your presence brings honor on this household. May I inquire as to the purpose of your visit?" The words in Aramaic belonged to a man in his sixties. His cloak was cut from dark brown goat's hair with a light cream-colored goat's hair trim at the sleeves and hem. A white beard covered most of his face, but the smile was warm and genuine.

Yeshai replied in Aramaic. He wanted to make sure that he was in the right place before revealing his identity.

"Is this the house of Hilkiah son of Shallum son of Zadok?"

"It is."

"Are you Hilkiah?"

"Blessed be the true Judge. He passed away from fever three days ago. I am Elimelech, his *m'chutan*—his father-in-law. Since he has no living relatives, I am here to take charge of his affairs on behalf of my daughter. May I ask who you are and what brings you to this house of mourning?"

Yeshai continued his introduction in Hebrew. "May the God of Abraham comfort you in your loss. I am Yeshai son of Gilad son of Eliezer, priest and scribe of the Judeans living in Samaria. I am Hilkiah's cousin. We are both descended from Achituv of Gezer."

The man called Elimelech fainted dead away. Yeshai rushed to offer aid but was pushed aside by a woman who appeared out of nowhere, wearing the garments of a mourner. He could not see her face, but he could feel her strength.

"Give us room, Persian. Don't touch him!" She practically shouted in Aramaic.

"I am not a Persian!" Yeshai replied in Hebrew.

"You are not Persian, and I am the widow of King David." The woman caught her breath as she realized that they were conversing in Hebrew.

"Who taught you to speak our tongue?" she asked, in a near whisper as she attempted to unfold her father and lay him flat on the ground.

"My parents, of course. As I was trying to explain to your father, I am a Judean from the community of exiles in Samaria. I am your husband's cousin, Yeshai son of Gilad."

"Then why are you dressed and bald as a Persian?"

"To save my life, but that is a very long story. Is your father all right?"

"If you are the cousin of my husband, then you are welcome in our home. But my father and I will demand proof that you are who you say you are. First, help me to carry him into the house."

After a few sips of cool water, Elimelech made a rapid recovery but was still having difficulty comprehending Yeshai's story.

"I see you have met my daughter, Ruth." Elimelech wiped beads of sweat from his forehead.

"That's not a Judean name, is it?"

"My mother was a daughter of Moab." There was a sharpness to her reply.

"I did not mean to make you angry. I merely asked."

"Ruth, go into the work room and bring us some papyrus and quill and ink. I want to see if this man is indeed a scribe as he claims."

"Of course, Father." In a moment she returned with the implements of a scribe. But Ruth did not bring a quill prepared for writing. Instead, she handed Yeshai a handful of feathers of various sizes and a small scribe's knife. She placed a clay inkpot and papyrus sheets on the wooden table before them. She watched Yeshai as he first examined each of the feathers and selected a single light brown one. With a few simple strokes of the very sharp knife, he cleared the shaft and held the quill in his hands to get a sense of the balance point before he made a cut and shortened the shaft. Then he fashioned a point. Her beloved Hilkiah worked the quills in exactly the same manner. But this proved nothing. He may have been a scribe, or at the very least, was taught how to write by a scribal master. It did not make him a relative.

Elimelech sought ways to expose Yeshai as a fake. "You say you are Hilkiah's cousin. How much then do you know of the story of the rescue of the sacred scrolls?"

"The story was told to me by my grandfather, Eliezer."

"Did your grandfather have any other brothers or sisters?"

"He had a twin brother Zadok who went into exile, here in Bavel."

"If you are a pretender, someone has instructed you well. Now write something that was contained in the sacred scrolls."

The thick ink was quickly absorbed into the dry papyrus sheet, but Yeshai began to put less and less ink on the tip of the quill. Elimelech glanced at Ruth. She was fixated on Yeshai's hands. There was no hesitation, no pausing to recall words of text with each stroke of the pen. Yeshai was writing from a deep-seated memory, not something he managed to learn in recent days. He filled the page with the Song of Moses at the Sea of Reeds. When he finished, he submitted his work to father and daughter for their inspection.

"Not only are you indeed a scribe of our people, but you are an artist as well," Elimelech said, unable to hide his admiration.

"That does not make him our kinsman," Ruth said.

"My Persian escort, the court official, Memukan, said that I bear a strong resemblance to your beloved husband, may peace be upon him. Look at me!"

Tears welled up in Ruth's eyes. She ran from the room.

"Your shaved head distorted your appearance for a while, but it was impossible to deny your resemblance to Hilkiah. You could have been twins. Dear cousin Yeshai, son of Gilad, the door of our home is open to you in blessing. I ask that you join us at our table tonight. You are welcome to stay with us for as long as your journey permits."

"I am not sure how long that will be. I am not even sure what I am doing here. Memukan made it seem as though the Emperor himself had ordered me to Hilkiah's house. But for what purpose, I do not know."

"There is an expression current among the Judeans in Bavel. 'The God of Israel commands and the Emperor acts.' I have no doubt that you have been sent by our God to this house to preserve and protect the sacred scrolls of our people."

"There is yet more to my story than what I have already shared with you. I spoke of my journey here, but I did not tell you the story of the twelve sacred scrolls that Eliezer my grandfather protected in Samaria."

For the next hour, Yeshai explained to Elimelech in great detail the story of the Judean priests in Samaria, the scribal school established by Eliezer, the mass copying of the scrolls, and finally, Eliezer's attempt to bring the twelve scrolls together in one single scroll.

"I am a simple Judean in the Exile. So, I may not understand the meaning of all you have told me. But I do know, with certainty, that God has sent you to this house. God has sent you to marry my daughter and give Hilkiah, peace be upon him, a son. You are the nearest, and it would seem only, living relative of Hilkiah ben Shallum. As a consecrated priest you understand that according to the laws of our people, it is your sacred duty to fulfill the obligation of the *Levir*, so that Hilkiah's name will not be erased from under heaven."

Yeshai was speechless. The pain of the loss of his own family was still an open wound that gave him no peace. Now he was about to be coerced into marrying a grieving widow to plant his seed, to produce an heir for the recently deceased cousin he never met.

"You must be exhausted from your journey. Take this reed mat to the roof of our home. Under the palm frond canopy you will find cool afternoon breezes that will aid in your rest. I will call you when it is time for the evening prayer."

"Living in Samaria, we Judeans prayed whenever we felt the need. What is the Evening Prayer?"

"Forgive me. You Judeans have the rebuilt Sacred House. We Judeans living in exile do not. We offer prayers each day at times that mark the sacrifices taking place in Jerusalem."

"I see," Yeshai said as he followed Elimelech to an external stairway that was at the rear of the house. The steps ended on a flat roof that matched the dimensions of the house below. On the west side of the roof was a square canopy with ample shade beneath. Yeshai unrolled the reed mat, set his leather saddle pouch on the ground next to it, then struggled to remove the Persian armor. As he was doing so, he caught sight of the small scroll visible from a corner of the pouch. He had forgotten the scroll, pressed into his hands at the last moment by the priest of Anatoth. He removed the scroll and then positioned the pouch to serve as a pillow beneath his head. Carefully, he unrolled the parchment and began to read: "*The words of Yeremiyahu son of Hilkiah, one of the priests at Anathoth in the territory of Benjamin.*" 'Benjamin' was the last word he was able to read before falling into a deep and undisturbed sleep.

CHAPTER THIRTEEN

DATE: March 19, 2009
TIME: 1:45 P.M. Local Time
PLACE: Tel Aviv District Police Headquarters, Shalma Street

S'gan Aluf Lavi met them at the front entrance security desk and provided his guests with access passes. Keller and Stone were asked to surrender their passports. Malik's ID was good enough to get him waived through.

Lavi offered assurance. "You'll get your passports back when you leave. They're safe with us. Follow me."

Instead of heading further into the building, Lavi turned around and walked out the front door and made a left turn at the street. They proceeded to walk into a quiet residential neighborhood that ran parallel to the District HQ. The area was dominated by stately semi-detached homes built in the 1930's and 40's. Lavi led them down the front path of the fourth house. Like others in the neighborhood, this one was a Bau Haus exemplar in a pastel green that looked rather handsome when contrasted with the cream-colored trim around the windows. He knocked lightly and a stocky woman with silver hair, wearing a frumpy housedress, opened the the solid oak door. She was about to speak but spotted Lavi and stepped aside. The police commander led the way to a door located beneath the stairway in the front hall.

"Was that woman going for the full Golda Meir look or what? Who lives here anyway?" Keller asked.

Lavi paused a few steps down on the stairway. "Her name is Olga, if you must know. Did you notice her left hand? It was wrapped around a Sig Sauer nine-millimeter with an expanded magazine. When we found out she was expelled from the Soviet GRU because she happened to be Jewish, we thought we might make use of her talents. She is a first-rate interrogator."

At the bottom of the carpeted stairway was an interior solid oak door with beautiful, highly polished brass hardware. Lavi slipped a plastic electronic key into a cleverly hidden slot built into the doorjamb. The door lock released and opened, revealing a long corridor. It had the look and feel of some sort of prison. The walls were grey concrete. Every four meters there was a heavy gage steel door.

"How many guests do you have today, Natan?"

"Only one, professor. Tovya Tsadka, the Samaritan council president. He wants to share some information with us."

"Did he always want to share this information, or did he have to be persuaded?" Stone asked.

Lavi gave a broad smile. "Fear not, Rabbi. He very much wants to cooperate. You can judge for yourself."

He led her, Malik, and Keller to the fourth door on the left-hand side of the corridor, where Tsadka was seated at a metal table. The Samaritan was wearing a plain white t-shirt and khaki slacks with a thin drawstring at the waist.

"Permit me to introduce you to Tovya Tsadka, leader of the Crown of Samaria – *Keter Shomron* and president of the Samaritan community council." Lavi introduced everyone to Tsadka. He used Keller's military rank in his introduction and did the same for Stone. She was beginning to wonder just when it was possible for Israelis to consider her a rabbi and when it was not. Only Omar the Druze insisted on calling her "Rabbi."

"No one was supposed to get hurt." Tsadka's English was fluent and clear. "You were not supposed to get hurt. I only agreed to scare you away from the Ezra Scroll so you would not be able to decipher its meaning. I want you to know that the murderers were not from my own people. They were not even hired by me."

Stone glared at Tsadka. "The apology and explanation will not restore a murdered family".

"I am acutely aware of that fact, Rabbi. And yes, I do know you are a rabbi. Professor Carlson is quite taken with you. He told me you were his best student."

"I don't give a damn what Carlson thinks of me!"

"Understood. I will grieve for that family every day of my life."

Without any preliminaries, Lavi began the questioning. "When did you first meet with Carlson?"

"About two years ago."

"Woa! Hold on there! I only found the scroll a few days ago," Keller said.

Lavi fixed Keller with a look of annoyance. "Let Tsadka continue, Sergeant. I believe you will find this fascinating. Not all of this violence is about your precious scroll."

Tsadka sought and received a nod from Lavi to continue.

"I met Carlson at the YMCA in Jerusalem. It was a Thursday afternoon, I think. I am not that sure about the date. Anyway, we had lunch."

"What was the stated purpose of the meeting?" Malik asked.

"Carlson said he was deeply interested in the history of the Samaritan Torah. He wanted to view our most ancient documents. I told him those were in East Lansing, at Michigan State University."

Malik leaned in. "Were you suspicious then?"

"Suspicious about what?"

"Suspicious about his lack of basic knowledge about the Samaritan Torah and its current location. Anyone sincerely interested should have known that."

"I wasn't at the time. He then requested access to the excavation of our ancient Temple on Mt. Gerizim."

"How did you respond?"

"Since he was a serious archeologist with glowing recommendations from colleagues, I thought that there was nothing wrong with granting him the access he requested. I told him that our council of elders would have to give their approval, but I thought it was a very doable request."

Lavi pushed. "Was that it?"

"No. He then asked to visit our communities in Holon and Nablus."

"Not just the archeological sites?"

"He claimed to want to get to know the people. I told him that I would put his request before the council. Since he was an American and not Jewish, I told him they were likely to approve his request. We set a date for his visits two weeks later. The council did approve, and the visits went off without a hitch."

Lavi produced a small notebook from his shirt pocket and consulted its contents. "What did he do during those visits to Nablus and Holon?"

"He took an extraordinary number of photographs with a large format digital camera. The elder who served as his guide in Nablus reported to me that he was doing very detailed studies of the site and the surface artifacts, as if he was trying to make a map of the topography."

"Then what happened?" Malik asked.

"Nothing. About a month or so passed, and then he called me and again asked to meet with me."

"What was that all about?" Stone joined in.

"He wanted to discuss with the elders of our community the possibility of conducting his own excavations on the site of the ancient Samaritan Temple."

"Did you agree to this request?" Lavi asked.

"All I could promise was to arrange for him to meet with the elders of the community."

Malik narrowed his eyes. "Was he satisfied with your answer?"

"Not really. No. In fact, he became quite hostile and agitated."

"How did you respond?" Malik asked.

"I responded the same way we Samaritans always respond to the outside world, when that world believes it has the right to treat our communities like museum pieces."

Stone piped up. "And what way is that?"

"I told him that permission for a special archeological excavation would require two things: a formal request from an accredited academic institution with an archeology program and a great deal of money."

Lavi continued. "And how did he take it?"

"He asked how much?"

"Just like that?" Malik asked.

"Yes, just like that."

Stone looked at Tsadka. "What did you tell him?"

"Twenty million Euros." A small smile broke out on Tsadka's face. "We Samaritans figure we should make the price for access high enough so that it will be worth the trouble the intrusion will bring."

"Then what happened?" Malik asked.

"Carlson just nodded his head, got up, and walked out of the restaurant. And that's when I knew that something was definitely not kosher."

Malik leaned back in his chair. "Why?"

"Professor, this is the Middle East. Carlson should have known that we were in the *Souq* – the market, as it were. If he was such a student of our culture, he should have countered with his own ridiculous number, say five hundred thousand. Negotiating a price in the Souq is second nature to us. It's in the very air we breathe. We love to haggle over the price of everything. I really got nervous when Carlson just nodded and left, like we had agreed to a number. It was way too easy."

Lavi was making notes. "What did you conclude from this?"

"I figured he was not doing this on his own. He had backers with very deep pockets."

"Then what did you do?" Stone asked.

"I went home and checked into Carlson's background."

Malik stood up and started to pace. "How did you do that?"

"I Googled him, looking for fundraising footprints."

"What did you find?" Keller asked.

"A single reference to a group called 'The Builders,' but there was absolutely no information about the group anywhere on-line. Pardon the pun, but that did not compute."

"What did you do next?" Lavi asked.

"The lack of on-line information about The Builders gave me an idea: I called Carlson and told him I knew who his backers were and that I needed to meet with them. I told him that my community could not risk putting the excavation of our most ancient and sacred sites in the hands of fanatics, terrorists, or amateurs."

"How did he respond?" Stone asked.

"After some perfunctory denials, he said he would arrange it and asked if the meeting could be held in the Old City, the next day. We agreed to meet for lunch at Papa Andrea's, a rooftop restaurant in the Christian Quarter. You can see the Church of the Holy Sepulcher from there."

"Tell us about that meeting," Malik asked. "We need as many details as you can remember."

"Can I get a fresh bottle of water, first?"

"No problem. This would be a good time for a break. Give us a few moments."

Lavi went out of the room, followed by Malik, Stone, and Keller. They took a few steps down the corridor and then circled close to one another.

Nodding toward Lavi, Malik said: "Tell us about The Builders."

"They are members of a secret society. We know very little about them."

"Are these guys Jews?" Keller asked.

"Far from it. Before we latched on to Tsadka, all we could piece together was that they are bedrock fundamentalist Christians, and that they are obsessed with preparing for the Second Coming of Christ."

"Why would they approach Samaritans?" Stone asked.

Lavi held out his arm in the direction of the cellblock, indicating it was time to return. "This you need to hear directly from Tsadka."

CHAPTER FOURTEEN

DATE: The Fourteenth Day of the Fourth Month, In the Seventy-first Year Since the Destruction of Jerusalem [515 BCE]
TIME: First Hour of the Second Watch
PLACE: Market Square, Pumbedita, Babylonia

Yeshai was in the third week of his personal exile in Bavel. He was a stranger among his own kin. There was so much he wanted to learn about his people, so many questions he wanted to ask. Taking daily meals with Ruth and Elimelech was an experience in awkward silence. The rare words they did exchange were confined to monosyllables.

In the absence of any conversation, Yeshai's imagination was his only faithful companion. That imagination was making him uncomfortable in Ruth's presence. He was having thoughts about her; imagining the female form that must have existed beneath the shapeless garments of her widowhood. Only the front half of her face was visible. What did her hair look like? He wondered. Was her skin darkened by the sun? Did she ever smile?

One evening, desperate for any measure of conversation, Yeshai sought to engage Elimelech in a discussion about his escape from Jerusalem and the reasons for his journey to Pumbedita. Elimelech waved those discussions aside, as if they were of no consequence. Instead, he wanted to know about Yeshai's life in Samaria, his family, his scribal skills, his prospects.

"My friends in the market tell me that you have become quite successful in providing scribal services."

"Mar Elimelech, my success is due, in no small measure, to you. I followed your advice and set up my table between the melon farmer and the woman who sells cucumbers. You were so right. The odor of freshly slaughtered goat meat was not conducive to people standing in line waiting for documents to be completed."

"So, you are making headway? People are coming to you?"

"They are! As they inspect the melons and fruit nearby, I can introduce myself to them and inform them about the lower fees I charge for scribal services."

Elimelech's shoulders slumped. "You can't make a living with lower fees."

Yeshai smiled. He knew where all of this was headed. "Are you concerned with my scribal business, or is there something else on your mind? Please do not misjudge me. I am grateful for the Persians rescuing me from certain death in Jerusalem. Memukan, the Pecha, seemed to believe that my presence in Bavel was part of some divine plan. Do you think that is so?"

Elimelech did not answer his question. "I am very tired. I am going to bed." He stood and left the room.

The next evening things were much the same. Ruth brought the simple meal to the table. In silence she placed each bowl in the center: rice, chickpea paste, and diced cucumbers. A moment later she returned with a plate filled with flatbread still warm from the clay brick oven. After Yeshai offered a brief prayer of thanksgiving, they began to eat. With a mouth full of food, Elimelech started to speak. Ruth admonished him with mock severity.

Elimelech cleared his throat. "Tell us about your family and life in Samaria."

Yeshai shook his head. "With all due respect, you have heard about me and my family three times over. Tell me about your family. Tell me about my cousin, Hilkiah."

"My family story is boring. Your cousin, Hilkiah, on the other hand was an orphan before his fourth year. The Great River Flood claimed his father, Shallum, and his mother, Aviva. His grandmother, Miryam, widow of Zadok, your great uncle, provided some stability in his chaotic life. She mentored him in scribal skills and took him into her confidence by telling him the complete version of their family story, including about the murder of Zadok.

"Having been trained as a scribe since his third year of life, Hilkiah would have been considered a worthy son-in-law for any Judean family. But being an orphan meant he had no family wealth to bring to the bridal canopy. To be honest, I took advantage of this situation to arrange a marriage for my daughter."

"Why would you have to do that? Yeshai spoke to Elimelech but never took his eyes off Ruth. Ruth kept her eyes low, fixed on the surface of the table before her.

Elimelech continued. "Look, I don't know how much you know about Judean life in Bavel. We like to think of ourselves as open and welcoming. It was important to be that way for our own safety. But, despite that openness, a daughter of a Moabite woman was still considered less than an ideal match. Fortunately, Hilkiah's mother's brother, Mechir, acted as his deceased parents' agent and quickly concluded the marriage pact. They were husband and wife for three short months before Hilkiah died of a fever."

Yeshai murmured, "Praised be the True Judge." It was now crystal clear to Yeshai that Ruth could become his wife if he took the next step. He knew that the traditions of Judah affirmed this. Yet he could not bring the words to his lips. Still, Yeshai knew that he would have to declare himself soon. Hospitality beneath Hilkiah's roof had its limitations, even for family.

Yeshai cleared his throat and looked directly at Elimelech. "Such a terrible loss. We have all suffered terrible losses. My own include a beautiful child and a loving wife. Death is a constant in life. The rules of family, clan, and tribe in our tradition exist to protect those who survive."

Elimelech raised his head and looked to his side at Ruth. "Are you ready to discuss your obligations as the *Yibum?*"

Yeshai nodded his head. "I am, if you and Ruth would have me in that role."

"You have no child of your own, yet you would do this? Ruth's voice startled Elimelech and Yeshai.

Yeshai faced her. "Yes, I know what it means to be cut off from my kin. Fulfilling my obligation as Hilkiah's nearest kinsman is my best chance to change that fact of my life."

"Even if the first child I bear after we are wed is Hilkiah's and not yours?"

"Yes, even so."

Elimelech stood at his place, looking directly at Ruth. "Our traditions make clear that you may not remarry before a full year has passed from the day Hilkiah died.

"Abba, I am well aware of the rules."

"There are relatives of Hilkiah on his mother's side of the family who are making claims at the seat of judgment in the city gates."

"What kind of claims?" Yeshai asked.

"They want this house and the land it sits on. They intend to sell it and make a quick profit."

"They are not asking for Ruth?" Yeshai's question sounded like a fearful pleading. Ruth faced Yeshai and saw him in a new light.

"Of course not. They have no obligations in that regard."

Yeshai knew this but wanted to make sure that the tradition did not have some local variation unique to Bavel.

"My only thought Ruth is for your security. If Yeshai is willing to make a public pronouncement now of his intention to fulfill his obligation as *Yibum* to Hilkiah, the possibility of Hilkiah's property going to that side of the family is ended. We must not wait for a year to pass for Yeshai to declare himself. That is all I am saying."

"Ruth, I make this declaration to you, here and now, that I will fulfill my obligation to my cousin Hilkiah and marry you when a full year has passed since the day of his death. I further acknowledge that, should the God of our ancestors bless us with children, the first child that is born will be Hilkiah's child in every respect. I promise that I will love you and provide for you as it is proper for a son of Judah to do for his bride."

Elimelech applauded. "Well said! It sounds like wedding contracts have been a specialty at your table in the market. There is only one problem."

"What's that?" Yeshai and Ruth spoke in unison then looked at each other in confusion.

"Yeshai's declaration means nothing until it is uttered in the presence of the people of the land at the city gate."

"Of course, we knew that." Again, they spoke in unison. Yeshai smiled, then laughed. Ruth smiled, then laughed. Elimelech's laughter could be heard out in the street. The room appeared brighter and warmer. Laughter had returned to the house of Hilkiah. In nine more months, it would become the house of Ruth and Yeshai.

One hour after dawn, the scruffy looking river raft managed to squeeze between two lengthy *kalaqs* already moored to the public landing at Pumbedita. The raft operator made his own lines fast, then waved his three passengers to climb the short stairway to the dock. His hand remained open in the direction of the passengers, silently appealing for an extra coin or two in appreciation for a safe journey.

Two of the departing passengers began to fumble with their draw-string purses in search of coins. The third passenger knocked their hands aside. There would be no extra coins. Grabbing the raft-man by his tunic, he hissed at him through clenched teeth. "You have been amply paid for this journey. That will be enough! Now we seek the leaders of the Judean exiles in Pumbedita. Direct us to them and you will get your coins."

The raft-man smiled and pointed to a low, square shaped brick building. "Go and ask at the customs house. They will know. I am not from here and have no idea how to find who you are looking for. May the stars and planets guide your journey."

Dov ben Asher and his two Levite soldiers gathered their belongings and made their way to the customs house.

"Ahem, excuse me. Do you work here?"

"What do you want?" rasped an ancient looking, thin-set man feigning sleep. He was propped up in a chair a few cubits away from the door to the customs house.

Without opening his eyes, the man in the chair responded. "By your accent I would say that you are Judeans from Judah. Why have you've returned to this Persian piss pot? Wasn't your life in the Province Beyond the Rivers luxurious enough for you?"

Dov ben Asher's two companions drew their bronze daggers.

"Easy there! I meant no disrespect. How can I help you travelers?"

Ben Asher stepped forward. "We are in pursuit of a fugitive from justice. He was our prisoner in Jerusalem."

"What was his crime?"

"Blasphemy."

"Persians might kill someone for insulting the emperor, but not for insulting a god. You will need to speak with your tribal kinsmen. They might help you. If you do find him, the Persians will not assist in his capture. They have too many gods to worry about insults to one or two of them."

"Then tell me how I can make contact with the *Pecha* for this area."

"You might be in luck. There is a session of the local court today. The *Pecha* usually attends to keep an eye on matters. Just follow this street which leads to the east and you will come to a market square."

"Thank you. What is your name?"

"I am called Bel."

Ben Asher brought out his coin purse and shook it so the jingle of coins could be heard. "Listen Bel, if you keep silent about our search, the gold is yours. If you do not, my men shall slit your throat and recover the gold."

Bel nodded his head in understanding. "Good luck with your search." He pulled himself up on his feet and watched as the Judeans headed for the city.

The proceedings of the Pumbedita city court took place out of doors. To the right side of the city gates, a raised platform was built for the purpose. On the platform were ten high-backed chairs. The chairs would be occupied by ten notables of the city, appointed by the Persian governor to act as a court of first resort. Routine legal disputes and contracts were handled by the "People of the Land". This was the standard venue for making legal notices in the presence of witnesses.

On most days, when the court was in session, twenty or thirty townspeople would gather to watch. As the session moved along, spectators would move in or out as their interest carried them. Today, there would be less people watching, because the Sabbath would arrive at sunset. Not all Judeans made an effort to observe the Sabbath, but those who did would be well away from the city gates by the time the sun was directly overhead. Yeshai was there to seek an opportunity to declare before the "People of the Land" his intent to marry Ruth under the venerable Judean rules of the *Yibum*.

Despite the approaching Sabbath, an unusually large crowd had gathered before the platform in anticipation of the airing of an ongoing dispute between a Persian carter and a Judean cloth merchant. The dispute consumed nearly two hours before its resolution.

Exhausted from the tedium of the proceedings, a well-dressed looking Persian, the leader of the day's session, was about to declare the meeting of the People of the Land over, when Yeshai sprang to his feet. "My lords," he proclaimed at the top of his lungs, "I have come today to declare before you my intention to marry Ruth, widow of the scribe Hilkiah, as soon as the days of her mourning are complete. In keeping with the traditions of our ancestors from Judah, I further declare that the firstborn of our union will be the son of Hilkiah in all matters of inheritance and family status. I freely undertake this obligation as the closest kin to Hilkiah, being the grandson of his grandfather's brother from Judah."

"Cannot this matter wait until our next session?" The Persian leader of the panel asked in frustration.

"With the greatest of respect, my lord, I must say it cannot."

"Why not?" asked a heavily bearded Judean on the platform.

"Because I am trying to prevent this body from assigning the property of my cousin to his relatives on his mother's side of the family. If you receive my declaration, it will put an end to their designs on his property and protect his widow. Hilkiah's name will be raised up by insuring he will have an heir."

"How do we know you are Hilkiah's real kinsman?"

"My lords, if I may speak?"

"Speak, Elimelech."

"I will vouch for his identity as Hilkiah's cousin."

"You are touched by the matter. You cannot provide testimony," the bearded Judean said.

"Then I shall vouch for his identity." A sudden quiet and all heads turned in the direction of the new speaker. It was the governor, Memukan, dressed in his official silk robes.

"This man is indeed Yeshai, grandson of Eliezer and great-grandson of Achituv, just as Hilkiah was. Among the exiles of Judah living in Samaria, he was their lead priest."

Yeshai bowed his head towards Memukan in gratitude.

Another Judean member of the People of the Land stood and spoke in a loud voice. "We have heard the testimony of our governor. Therefore, in keeping with the traditions of our people, the exiles of Judah, we acknowledge the claim of Yeshai son of Gilad as the nearest relative of Hilkiah, son of Shallum. He has made his promise to fulfill the obligation of the nearest kinsman of his cousin and in so doing raise up his name in the household of Judah. Furthermore, Elimelech is appointed the guardian of Hilkiah's property until Yeshai shall marry Hilkiah's widow."

"Do the People of the Land agree in this decision?"

"We do!" they shouted in unison, eager to leave.

Yeshai immediately approached Ruth and Elimelech. He reached for Ruth's hand, gave it a gentle squeeze as he looked directly into her eyes. They were filled with tears. He did not know if they were tears of mourning or joy. He knew that the tears welling up in his own eyes were of joy. He intended to linger in that moment, but a heavy hand rested on his shoulder and directed him to turn away from Ruth.

"I must speak with you--now!" The order came from an elderly Judean, his head covered in the manner of the priests and Levites, his hands stained black from the thick ink of scribes.

Yeshai narrowed his gaze. "And you are?"

"I am Meremot son of Uriah, the current guardian of the sacred scrolls of Judah in Exile."

CHAPTER FIFTEEN

DATE: March 19, 2009
TIME: 2:50 P.M. Local Time
PLACE: A Safe House Near Tel Aviv Police Headquarters

Tsadka leaned back and stared into space. The stress of the interrogation had clearly exhausted him. Dark shadows dominated his face. "When can I speak with a lawyer and call my family?"

Lavi smiled briefly. "If you continue to answer our questions truthfully, this session should not take too much longer."

Malik stood over Tsadka. "You were going to tell us about your meeting with Carlson and his benefactors in the Old City. Were they the 'Builders'?

Tsadka nodded then closed his eyes, trying to remember the details of his exchange with Carlson. "It was a beautiful and clear Friday in October. I believe that the Jewish High Holy Days had just concluded. The Old City had returned to its normal quotient of tourists, which meant that the restaurants in the Christian quarter were nearly empty. Carlson was seated with two men on the western edge of the rooftop restaurant. As I approached their table, I could see the empty narrow streets below. A couple of Christian gift shops were open. Just as I was sitting down, the bells from a nearby church clock tower began tolling the noon hour. At that very moment, the loudspeakers in the Muslim Quarter began sounding the Friday call to prayer. You might say it was a very interfaith moment. Carlson introduced his guests to me."

"Describe them please," Lavi said.

"The first, who I took to be the leader, was Reverend Jones. He looked to be about sixty-five or seventy, with a stocky build. I would guess he was nearly two meters in height, but he remained seated the whole time, so I'm not totally sure. He had piercing blue eyes and a thick head of wavy, white hair. He was clean-shaven and badly sunburned." Tsadka paused. "Oh, and he spoke with what you Americans call a Southern accent."

"Now how would you know that?" Keller asked.

"I spent two years as a student at Michigan State University in East Lansing, Michigan. It was a very diverse campus. I heard all kinds of accents."

"Why Michigan State?"

"Do you have the time to listen to the explanation?"

Malik shrugged. "It might be relevant. Let's see where it leads."

"As leader of the Samaritan community, it was my duty, like my father before me, to study our sacred texts. I know it sounds strange, but those sacred texts are housed at Michigan State University. The texts were discovered by researchers studying the Samaritan religion in the 1950's and donated to Michigan State. Given the dwindling size of our community and the volatility of Near Eastern politics, our community never sought the repatriation of that library. But our community has unrestricted access to the collection."

"Is that where you learned English?" Stone asked.

Malik decided that the Michigan State connection was not relevant. "Could we get back to the meeting? Describe the second man."

Tsadka looked over to Lavi and received a nod. "I think he is the son of the older gentleman, though they were introduced with different last names--Reverend Jones was the older guy and Reverend Smith was the younger one. I am sure these were fake names."

"You think? Please describe Reverend Smith."

"He had the same piercing blue eyes as Jones. That's why I thought they were related. He appeared to be a quarter meter taller. His skin was tanned, but it looked artificial. He was a *ring-nik.*

"A what?" Keller asked.

"It's an Israeli term for American men who love to wear flashy rings," Lavi explained.

"Can you describe the rings?" Malik asked.

"He wore a solid gold wedding band with no adornment and a wide band with a large diamond on the pinky of his left hand. On his other hand was an even bulkier ring with a large blue stone. It had images of buildings on both sides of the band. Oh yes, and there was a gold cross inlaid into the blue stone. They were so large they were hard to ignore."

"Tell us about the details of your meeting," Lavi said.

"They started off by trying to blackmail me."

"How so?"

"Reverend Jones threatened to expose our money smuggling operations on the West Bank. He showed me the business card of an Israeli Police Major. He said it would be simple for him to place a call and have half of my community locked up."

"What else?"

"He warned me not to reveal anything about this meeting—he said they knew where I live and I'd be dead in less than twenty-four hours if I spoke to the police.

"As incredible as this sounds, they told me that they were going to blow up the Dome of the Rock."

Keller started to pace the room. "This makes absolutely no sense. He barely knows you and yet he begins by telling you a secret that can get him a life sentence for terrorist activity."

"I am still unsure of why he did that, unless it was to impress me with his power and ruthlessness. I do believe there was an implied threat contained in this revelation—you know, something like, if we are willing to anger a few hundred million Muslims, imagine what we could do to your tiny group of Samaritans if you dare to cross us."

Stone shook her head in disgust. "And Smith and Jones call themselves Christians."

Lavi motioned for Tsadka to continue. "Go on."

Tsadka tried to convince him. "They believe that God has come to them in a vision and instructed them to build the third Temple, after which their Savior, Jesus Christ, will return and save the faithful. They claimed to have allies in the Ultra-Orthodox Jewish communities, as well. The 'Ultra's' role in the drama will be to start a civil war between Orthodox and secular Jews. At the same time, The Builders intend to hold the Church of the Holy Sepulcher hostage while the construction is taking place. If they are left alone, the church will survive. If not, they will blow it up."

Stone was incredulous. "Did Jesus tell them to blow up anything and anyone that opposes them? What does this have to do with the Samaritans and their ancient temple?"

"The Builders believe that the Samaritan Temple was identical to the first version of the Second Temple. They wanted to measure the ancient Samaritan Temple to get the design just right. I guess Jesus won't return if the Third Temple is shoddy."

"Did you believe that they intended to carry out this scheme?" Malik asked.

"It all sounded so crazy, so no, I didn't at first, but as they were talking, I became aware of their attention to detail, their meticulous planning. That was when I thought to myself, they are really going to do this!"

Now it was Stone's turn to pace. "If they had the ability to kill or blackmail you, why did they decide to pay you off instead?"

"They may have been just blowing smoke, but they said they needed our cooperation and talents for the success of their project. In their eyes we Samaritans have many defects, but we have great local connections and the ability to move things back and forth freely between Israel, the West Bank, Syria, and Lebanon. They cannot succeed without us acting as facilitators."

Lavi faced Malik. "The Builders got on our radar a few years ago. They are amazing fundraisers. They used their official church identity, The Church of the Risen Christ, and public outlets to gather and wash their proceeds. With their TV shows and stadium concerts they can raise billions from the gullible, the hopeless and the hopeful."

Stone was angry. "If you join limitless funds with religious fanaticism, you have a dangerous mix. Didn't you see that?"

Tsadka looked at the floor. "I naively thought that we could use their wealth to our advantage without causing damage to our community."

Keller raised his voice and directed it to Lavi. "How come these guys were able to fly under your world-class intelligence operation radar?"

"Christian fundamentalists are far down on the list of threats being assessed."

"Maybe it's time to move them up the list."

"They are big donors to our right-wing parties. It causes a certain amount of willful blindness."

"What did they want from you, then and there?" Malik asked.

"They wanted to set up a materials distribution center within our community in Nablus. They were going to finance the building of immense underground warehouses out of solid rock for the storage of materials for building and explosives for demolition. Our under-employed Samaritan youth would be put to work at going rates. They wanted me to say yes to the plan and then sell it to the community elders as an economic development plan for our entire community."

"Did you say yes?" Malik asked.

"I said I would have to think about it and get back to them. Selling their plan to the elders would not be easy. I asked for time."

"Did they give you time?" Stone asked.

"They gave me six months to make it happen. Then, a week ago, they called and told me that they had a problem that could cause the entire project to collapse. Their problem was you and Sergeant Keller, and the scroll he found."

"Who, specifically, were you talking to?" Lavi's voice rose.

"The reverends Smith and Jones were both on the line. They claimed that Professor Carlson had just examined an ancient scroll that could lead to the discovery of an original Torah among the Samaritans, one older than the oldest biblical text known to be in existence. The reverends were fearful that such a text would undermine claims of divine authorship for the Torah. Since for most Christians, the truth of Jesus' divine nature is based on acceptance of the divine authorship of Torah, such a discovery would have a devastating effect on Christian fundamentalists. They asked me to arrange for a few accidents that would turn Keller and Stone away from their pursuit of the original Torah."

"A bomb is no accident," Stone said.

"Bombs go off all the time around here. It was supposed to be a weak bomb, meant to scare, not to kill. How totally naive of me to think I had things under control. The Palestinian men I hired saw this as an opportunity to do more than superficial damage."

"So, you did agree to carry out their request for accidents?" Malik charged.

"I did, but then I made a side deal with Carlson."

"What kind of side deal?" Keller asked.

"As soon as the Reverends hung up, Carlson called me back. He wanted to give me information about the travel plans of the Rabbi and the Sergeant, so I could arrange the necessary accident. Then he mentioned that he was in possession of the actual scroll. I made him an offer. Ten million Euros for the Ezra scroll."

"You intended to pay Carlson with half of the money you were getting from the Reverends?" Stone asked.

"Precisely. I just could not let them destroy such an essential piece of my people's heritage. I was going to buy it on behalf of my community. It could lead to a discovery that would insure our very survival."

"So now we know that the Builders are dead set against the discovery of that so-called original Torah," Lavi said. "We also know that, for the moment, they are unaware that the Ezra scroll is safely in our hands."

"There is just one more thing," Tsadka said, "though I am not sure if this is important."

"What might that be?" Stone asked.

"As I approached the table for our meeting, I noticed the two reverends stuffing a stack of tourist maps and brochures into their backpacks."

"So?" Malik asked.

"During our meal, my napkin fell off of my lap and when I bent down to retrieve it, I noticed one of the brochures on the floor. Parts of it were highlighted in bright yellow."

Stone stared at Tsadka. "What site was described in the brochure?"

"The Shrine of the Book."

CHAPTER SIXTEEN

DATE: The Fifteenth Day of the Fourth Month, In the Seventy-first Year Since the Destruction of Jerusalem
TIME: Third Hour of the Second Watch
PLACE: Before the City Gates, Pumbedita, Bavel

"Meremot son of Uriah, what is so important that it cannot wait until the end of shabbat? If you happened to pay attention to the proceedings today, then you know that our family has much to celebrate."

But Meremot would not be deterred. "Your cousin Hilkiah assigned me a task and I must fulfill it. I gave my personal oath to him. It was his last wish before he died. He instructed me to give you this letter." Meremot placed a small scroll bound with coarse thick twine in Yeshai's hand.

"Now that you have fulfilled your oath, I wish you peace."

Meremot smiled and fixed Yeshai with a piercing gaze. "My young friend, do not be in such a hurry. When you read this scroll, you will need one additional piece of information. The meeting will take place at sunset on the first day of the coming week at the house of Elias, son of Yehochanan." Without waiting for Yeshai to respond or ask questions, Meremot turned away and disappeared into the crowded marketplace.

"What meeting?" Yeshai's question hung in the air. He decided he would not let Hilkia's message from beyond the grave spoil the celebration of his betrothal to Ruth. He put the scroll in the pocket of his tunic and with a bounce in his step, started walking home.

The aroma of roasted lamb with herbs and spices hit him when he opened the door. It was glorious. Now, Yeshai understood Elimelech's late arrival at the city gate. He was organizing and preparing the shabbat feast. The meal was wonderful. The conversation at the table had a comfort level that was usually reserved for close friends and family. When the table had been cleared, Elimelech poured an extra cup of sweet thick wine for each of them.

"I am a happy man. My daughter is protected. My son-in-law, peace be upon him, is protected, and I shall also be the *chotein*, to a famous scribe of Samaria. With any luck at all before I die, children shall call me *Sabba*."

Ruth laughed. "Abba!"

"Listen to yourself. Only a few days ago you were disconsolate about your future because you had none. Now everything is possible. This would be a good time for me to share with Yeshai a story about you when you were a little girl.

"Abba, don't you dare!"

"I only thought that since there was still nearly an hour of oil left in the lamps, we might continue to enjoy each other's company a little while longer before we have to turn in. Besides, now that your wedding has been publicly announced, your future husband should know more about his betrothed."

In that particular moment of joy and happiness, Yeshai remembered an ancient Judean superstition. "Evil spirits lurk in the shadows of joy." Was his encounter with the old scribe in the marketplace a sign of evil spirits lurking? Perhaps this was his opening to mention Meremot and the message from Hilkiah.

Yeshai cleared his throat. "Oh, that reminds me, the strangest thing happened at the city gates."

Ruth turned her attention to Yeshai.

"Just when the court session was concluded, an old man approached me with this." Yeshai produced the scroll from the pocket of his robe and described his conversation with Meremot.

"Perhaps it is time to read Hilkiah's message," Elimelech offered.

"Then Yeshai should do so privately. My late husband went to a great deal of trouble to make sure he would receive this letter. Maybe it is not meant for anyone else's eyes but his."

Yeshai shook his head. "Please forgive my directness. I will not keep secrets from you or your father. Secrets breed suspicion and unhappiness. We must learn to trust one another in all matters. We should begin to do so now, here."

"So be it."

Yeshai unrolled the small scroll. It was two sheets, one inside the other. The letter was written on a material pressed and formed from the stalks of reeds, found in abundance along the banks of every river in lower Bavel. The writing was flowing, as if without pause or hesitation. Yeshai was not surprised to see that the form of each letter followed the scribal traditions of Judah, as taught in the last days of the Sacred House before the exile. As he examined the message, he had the growing sense that the shape of the letters was a special bond that connected all members of his family.

Dear Cousin:

If you are Yeshai son of Gilad son of Eliezer son of Achituv from Gezer, and you are reading these words, then what I have feared most has come to pass. I am making my journey to Sheol, leaving my beautiful wife, Ruth, a widow. Only Ruth and her devoted father know the truth. I have been poisoned, slowly over time, but poisoned nonetheless...

"Is this true?" Yeshai said. "Did you know this? Why didn't you tell me?" "Read the letter and then we will talk," Elimelech said. But know this, we are all in danger." Shaking his head, Yeshai continued to read aloud.

How I know this to be true is of little consequence now. What matters is the protection of the sacred scrolls of Judah. The path of your life and mine have never intersected but they have been marked by many of the same boundary stones: scribe, priest, guardian of the Sacred Scrolls.

Six months before I put ink to this scroll, during a single week, every single hair on my body fell out. A year earlier, I witnessed the slow and painful death of a close friend. It began in the exact same manner. I knew then that I did not have long to live. I had to prepare for my certain death. Without an heir, the safety and preservation of the Sacred scrolls would become the responsibility of the very people who were killing me. It should be clear now that fulfilling our task, and upholding our oath to protect the scrolls, will be dangerous. My death will be proof that our exiled community is divided into factions, and at least one of these factions is willing to kill those who oppose them. I needed a plan that would expose their evil.

My first step was to entreat the Persian Pecha, Memukan, to locate you and bring you to Pumbedita. For many years he has been a true friend of the House of Judah, doing more than is necessary to sustain Judeans in exile, as well as the community of returnees now in Judah. Your arrest in Samaria was not an accident. The reach of the poisoners is long. It extends from Bavel to Judah to Samaria. As you were the publicly acknowledged guardian of the Sacred scrolls preserved in Samaria, they had to find a way to take them from you. You had to be disgraced and murdered to enable their plans to succeed. And what is it they seek that they will commit murder to achieve? They seek to throw off the yoke of Persia, build an opulent Sacred House and place a descendant of David on the throne. As consecrated priests, they will build their own Judean empire on the free will offerings of the poor. They can do this because they possess the Mishkan scroll. Elimelech and Ruth will explain to you about the abomination known as the Mishkan. The scrolls you protect are the only proof that the Mishkan scroll is not the work of the God of Moses but rather the clever lies of the false prophet, Ezekiel.

You must be present at the next gathering of the Scribes of Judah In Exile. If you are reading this letter, it means that Meremot son of Uriah has informed you of the time and place of that gathering. You may trust him. Put your trust also in Ruth and her father, Elimelech. They will guide you. They know who is true to our tradition and who is false.

My final prayer is that you will fulfill the obligation of the levir, marry Ruth, and sire my son. Thus, the house of Achituv will continue and my name will not be blotted out from under heaven. Please love her and care for her. She is as much a daughter of Judah as my mother and grandmother were.

May the peace of our God be upon us all.

Hilkiah son of Shallum-Hacohein v'hasofer.

The letter bore a puddle of red wax. The imprint of a cylinder-seal had been rolled across the wax when it was pliable. The impression was identical to a broken cylinder-seal Yesahi had noticed suspended from a leather thong around Ruth's neck. When Yeshai looked up from the scroll he saw large tears welling up in Ruth's eyes. She turned away from his gaze and wiped her eyes. Elimelech tried but failed to clear his throat. He too was overwhelmed. Yeshai wanted answers. He could not wait for these emotions to pass. He needed answers now.

"Who is poisoning us and how is he doing it?"

Elimelech's eyes narrowed. "Not 'he,' they. They are poisoning us!"

"All right, who are they?"

"They are members of the priestly clan of Ezekiel." Elimelech cleared his throat properly this time and began his lengthy explanation. "The first leader of the exiles of Judah in Bavel was a priest and prophet named Ezekiel ben Buzzi. He is the one who divided the sacred scrolls and sent twelve of them with your grandfather Eliezer, into hiding in Samaria. The other twelve accompanied the exiles to Bavel. In time, Hilkiah's grandfather, Zadok, became the guardian of the scrolls in Bavel. As our exile community settled into a normal life of sorts, this Ezekiel took for himself the title of High Priest and became like a father to Zadok."

Over the course of the next hour, with their worried faces reflected in the yellow glow of the Sabbath oil lamps, Elimelech and Ruth relayed the story of Zadok's discovery of the *Mishkan* scroll; the construction of the *Mishkan* in Bavel; Zadok's realization that the *Mishkan* scroll was actually written by Ezekiel; the murder of Zadok; the flood that destroyed the *Mishkan* and caused the death of Shallum and Aviva, Hilkiah's father and mother; the strength of Miryam in raising Hilkiah and preserving the scribal tradition; and finally the Persian conquest of Bavel and the apparent end of the exile.

Yeshai stood and started to pace the room. "One day I must tell you of the Judean exiles in Samaria and our own efforts to preserve the sacred scrolls, but I am overwhelmed with questions from your story. I must begin with the most important question of all, how are you being poisoned?"

"We only know that it is from our food or water. Perhaps it is from everything we eat, drink or touch," Ruth said.

"It must be something else. Only Hilkiah was affected." Perhaps we begin by speaking with Meremot.

"My next question has to do with your service of the God of our ancestors. You have no Sacred House. Do you worship at all?"

Elimelech sipped wine from his cup. "When the *Mishkan* was destroyed, Ezekiel died with it. For a brief time, the exiles of Judah were united in viewing these events as a sign from God that a great sin had been committed. Ezekiel's loyal followers, priests and Levites who were powerful in the days when the *Mishkan* stood, were desperate to maintain their power and status. They continued to use the *Mishkan* scroll as a sign of priestly authority over the exiles. They managed this even without a place of worship. They continued to elect a High Priest and organized themselves into watches. They paraded around in priestly garb and extorted gifts from the poor on the promise that their sacrifices would be pleasing to God."

Ruth refilled their cups, then continued. "They knew that the people would not tolerate another *Mishkan* in Bavel, so they offered sacrifices in the courtyard of the home of the High Priest. The priests taught the people that as soon as the Sacred House was restored in Judah, they would end the sacrifices in Bavel. But the followers of Ezekiel only spoke of rebuilding the Sacred House. They prophesied and dreamt about its dimensions, its materials, its splendor. This is how they raised money in Bavel for the reconstruction in Judah. But the money never got there."

Elimelech's voice rose in anger. "Travelers from Jerusalem brought reports to our community. For nearly twenty years after the exile had ended, no one in Jerusalem was raising a beam or a wall for a new Sacred House. There were so many divisions among the Judeans competing for power in Judah. You saw them for yourself: Judeans returning from their exile in Bavel engaged in combat with Judeans who remained behind in Judah; Judean refugees in Samaria, like yourself, seeking to return to Jerusalem and the restoration of the Sacred House. Ezekiel's priestly kin grew rich during their exile in Bavel. While blaming the tribes of Edom, Ammon, Moab, and Samaria for preventing construction of the Sacred House, they had no intention of returning to Zion. They insisted that God would decide when it was time to build."

Ruth continued telling the story. "Perhaps God did decide, after all. Darius, Emperor of Persia ordered the priests of Judah to rebuild or return the gold, silver, and bronze artifacts that had been given them by Cyrus. Only then did the clan of Ezekiel begin preparations to return to Judah and undertake an actual rebuilding of the Sacred House."

"So where do you and the rest of the Judean exiles in Bavel worship?"

"Some of us worship in our homes and sometimes in places of meeting."

"Do you offer sacrifices at these meetings?"

"Certainly not!" Ruth said.

"We only know for certain what takes place here in Pumbedita. Most of those who gather for these meetings are scribes and their families. We are fortunate to be in the town where the sacred scrolls are kept. The Guardians of the Scrolls will bring forth one or more of the scrolls and read them to the people. The people will praise God for the words on the scrolls and for keeping the people together, even in exile."

"How many Judeans are at these meetings and how often do they take place?"

"We do not take a count. That would be an affront to God. You will see for yourself at the gathering the day after tomorrow. We meet whenever we can be sure that the clan of Ezekiel is not watching. The first day of the coming week is a festival day for the Persians. Ezekiel's clan has been invited to the governor's palace to join in the celebration. Let's just say that we were able to arrange the invitation for them."

Ruth spoke with a vehemence Yeshai had never heard before. "You must take up the cause of the scrolls where Hilkiah had been stopped."

"My leadership of the Judeans in Samaria is going to work against me. The Guardians will not be pleased to learn that the Samaritans took possession of the Sacred Scrolls from my grandfather. How can they trust a scribe who is an accomplice to the loss of sacred texts. How can they trust me to guard the remaining twelve scrolls?"

More importantly, Yeshai thought to himself, what will they do when the find out about the hidden scroll?

The remaining oil in the last lamp still giving light, sputtered out. There was darkness and there was silence.

"It's time we turned in. There's much to think about tomorrow, before shabbat ends," Yeshai said.

CHAPTER SEVENTEEN

DATE: March 19, 2009
TIME: 3:15 P.M. Local Time
PLACE: Café Michal, 230 Dizengoff Street, Tel Aviv

Keller surveyed the cafe patrons at surrounding tables, checking for eavesdroppers. His voice was filled with tension. "Look, I'm as hungry and thirsty as the next person, but why are we sitting here ordering lunch when a couple of crazies are plotting to destroy The Shrine of the Book? Is the security in your office so bad that you need to sit in a sidewalk café to avoid listening devices?"

Lavi smiled. "Sergeant, it's a beautiful spring day. The food is good here and I think better when I am not distracted by the noises of my office. Besides, we have no evidence that The Builders intend to blow-up The Shrine of the Book. Maybe they were just being tourists with that brochure. Visiting the Dead Sea Scrolls is what tourists and fundamentalists do when in Jerusalem. We should keep our focus on locating the Bone Box."

Malik's eyes appeared focused on his menu, but his mind was turning over the details of their interrogation of the Samaritan leader, Tsadka. "What do you really know about Reverends Smith and Jones?" He asked Lavi.

Lavi withdrew an unmarked blue folder from his metal briefcase. He flipped a few pages over and then began reciting. "Their real names are Ervin and Lemuel Rumsey. They are indeed father and son. Reverend Ervin is the son of an Alabama sharecropper, whatever that is."

"It means he came from a family that was very poor," Keller said.

"Anyway, he quit school in the seventh grade to help his father grow pecans. When he was fifteen, his parents' house or shack or whatever you call it, caught fire in the middle of the night. Both parents died, but Ervin survived. The fire was suspicious, but no charges were ever filed.

"Ervin was taken under the wing of his family pastor, Reverend Silas Mercer, who got him back in school and ultimately paid for his education at Bob Jones University in Greenville, South Carolina, and Ervin was ordained a Southern Baptist minister in 1975. In 1985, he founded The Church of the Risen Christ, in Eldorado, Arkansas. The Church grew and eventually moved to Shreveport, Louisiana. There, Ervin met and married the seventeen-year-old daughter of a church elder. They had one child, a son, Lemuel. The wife died trying to give birth to their second child, a stillborn daughter. The son, Lemuel, was a prodigy, at least when it came to preaching."

Lavi checked to see if his companions were paying attention then continued to read from the file. "By 1990, The Church of the Risen Christ had a very slick TV show that led in the ratings for religious broadcasting six years in a row. The show brought in millions in donations."

"So Tsadka was not exaggerating. These guys do have the capacity to raise the money for such an operation," Keller said.

Lavi cleared his throat. "Big donors were admitted into an exclusive club—The Builders—with regular access to the great preacher. The membership roster of The Builders was a closely guarded secret. Then, suddenly, in late September 2001, The Builders simply disappeared."

"What do you mean disappeared?" Malik asked.

"It was as if the very mention of them was erased from Church documents and outlets. They vanished from all publications, broadcasts and internet materials produced by the Church of the Risen Christ. It was as if they had never existed."

"They must have gone underground," Keller said.

"We do not know when, where, or how their ideology or mission changed. Carlson's direct contact with the two reverends is the first time anything about The Builders has surfaced since 2001. Smith and Jones never used the name. Carlson is the one who used the term."

Stone was working the problem. "If The Builders were so secret, how did Carlson come to know about them?"

Lavi closed the file. "Probably the same way our analysts built the file. They Googled the Rumseys and drew conclusions. Carlson is no dummy. Actually, this stuff is very fresh.

Some interviews were conducted with people who may have known them ten years ago in South Carolina."

"Professor, do you buy all this stuff about rebuilding the Temple?" Stone asked.

"Given the number of crazies, Israelis and evangelicals who believe that God has called them to rebuild the Temple, I would not be surprised if one or another of them was taking steps to see such a plan to fruition. What I do not buy is Tsadka's leaping to the conclusion that The Builders want to destroy the Shrine of the Book as well." Malik closed his eyes and began stroking his chin.

"Why not?" Stone asked.

"Motive. Why would they do such a thing? Most Christians view the exhibits in The Shrine of the Book as confirming the historicity of the New Testament. For them the Dead Sea Scrolls are witness to an incredibly long and faithful tradition of scribal transmission for the Hebrew Scriptures. Except for one or two heresies that broke out in the formative period of Christianity, most denominations acknowledge a deep spiritual connection to the Torah, the Prophets, and the Writings of the Hebrew Scriptures. Even the most dedicated of Christian fundamentalists see the Hebrew Scriptures as essential prophecies foretelling the arrival and mission of Jesus."

Malik resettled himself in his chair and rearranged the silverware at his place. "Despite all of the fantasy and media hype, the Shrine of the Book's collection has not contradicted one sentence of the Hebrew Scriptures. To put it crassly, the Red Sea still parts and the Israelites still walk on dry land. With the glaring exception of the Book of Esther, all the rest of the books of the Hebrew Scriptures are present and accounted for in the Dead Sea Scrolls. The Builders gain nothing by destroying the Shrine of the Book."

When the meal arrived, everyone became lost in their own thoughts and food. After ten minutes had passed, Keller proposed an answer to Malik's question of motive.

"Professor, what if destroying the Shrine is not religious but political?"

"Meaning?"

"Suppose the purpose is to discredit Israel's stewardship of the Dead Sea Scrolls. Remember the accusations of anti-Semitism and favoritism leveled at the original Scroll scholars?"

"How do you know this stuff?" Stone asked.

"I know all about the controversy surrounding the Scrolls. There were multiple controversies connected with their ownership, discovery, meaning, and the right to read and publish scholarly articles."

"And you know this how?" Lavi challenged.

"I wrote a report on the Scrolls for my Bar Mitzvah project."

"You have got to be kidding." Stone laughed.

"I'm deadly serious. It was because of that report I was able to recognize the Paleo-Hebrew script of the Ezra scroll. Anyway, if major artifacts and scrolls were destroyed in a terror attack it would start a groundswell of anti-Israel agitation and international outcry."

"Resulting in what?" Malik asked.

"The removal of the scrolls from Israel's control altogether."

"That's not going to happen, not ever," Lavi said.

"What if The Builders have already figured out the location of the *Sefer Torat Moshe?*" Stone asked. "The attack on the Shrine could be a diversion. They blow it up and while a massive emergency response is underway, with hundreds of police, medics, and archeologists rushing to the Shrine to save lives and preserve priceless scrolls, they make their move to steal the original Torah."

Malik nodded his head in agreement. "Rabbi, you are on to something. That would mean that The Builders are way ahead of us. They think they know where the bone box of Shoshana bat Talmon is."

"So, we have to locate the box and get there before The Builders do and steal it from under their noses," said Keller.

"That is brilliant Sergeant! So where is the bone box? Malik asked.

"I haven't got a clue."

"Actually, we do have a clue," Lavi said. "For a diversion to work, the thieves need to be certain that the police and emergency services are fully engaged with the bombing. They will also need to be able to communicate with one another via two-way radio."

"Why not use their cell phones?" asked Keller.

"In the event of a terror attack, which is what this will feel like, the mobile networks will be jammed with calls. The thieves cannot risk being out of touch with one another. Thus, the diversion cannot be across town or across the country from the main event. Too many things could interfere with their transmission. The two sites will be close to one another."

"How close, Colonel?"

"Less than two miles, I would say."

Stone grabbed a paper napkin from a holder, opened it and spread it out in the center of the table. With a pen left by their server, Stone drew a circle in the center and pointed. "If the Shrine of the Book is in the center and the two-mile point is the circle, the scroll must be in a building somewhere inside the circle. So, what buildings would be a likely location for precious artifacts?"

Malik picked up the pen from the table and drew two stars roughly half the distance from the center, one North and one South. "This star," he explained, pointing to the star below the center, "is the Israel Museum. And this star," he said, pointing to the star above the center, "is the Israel Museum lab and storage facility. If the bone box is close to the Shrine of the Book, my money is on it being in the lab and storage facility."

"Is there any way we can know for sure? The Builders must have been able to follow some kind of trail," said Stone.

"Excuse me for being dense but I still don't get what The Builders want from the original Torah," Keller said.

"What if Israel drowns in the Red Sea in the original Torah?" Stone asked.

"Huh?"

"What I mean is, what if The Builders are afraid that the original is different from the Torah we have now, in some fundamental way?"

"Go on," Malik said.

"So, let's say that there is an essential idea in Christianity that is based on some concept in the Torah but is downplayed or is nowhere to be found in the original Torah."

"Like what?" Lavi asked.

"Atonement through sacrifice." Stone folded her hands. "Did I ask you for sacrifices in the wilderness?"

"What is that supposed to mean?" Keller asked.

Malik explained. "The prophet Jeremiah poses this question and implies that whatever the Israelites are doing in the Temple of Solomon, God did not command it."

Stone nodded. "That passage has always troubled me. Jeremiah, speaking on behalf of God, is almost offhand about the comment, as if everyone knows it to be true but is unwilling to say so out loud. Sacrifices appear throughout the Torah, even in sections determined to be from non-priestly authors," Stone said. "I am never sure what Jeremiah's point, or rather God's point, is."

"What do you mean, 'non-priestly' authors?" Keller asked.

"Do you remember what I said about the so-called Documentary Hypothesis?" Malik asked.

"Yeah, so?"

"According to that hypothesis, the newest material in the Torah is from the time of Ezra in Babylonia, around the year 443 BCE. That newer material includes the entire book of Leviticus and major sections of Exodus. Even though there are passages throughout the rest of the Torah that have been identified as 'priestly,' it is very clear that the entire Book of Leviticus was written by the *cohanim*—the priests. They place a heavy emphasis on the atoning value of sacrifice and the importance of achieving that atonement through a sacrificial cult operated exclusively by the descendants of Aaron. The older material in the Torah, according to the hypothesis, came from non-priestly sources."

Keller's eyes lit up. "I get it. Leviticus is relatively new and adds the idea of killing animals to atone for sin. But what has this got to do with Christians?"

"When the Romans destroyed the Temple in 70 CE, all surviving Jewish sects, including followers of Jesus, were left in a serious quandary. With the Temple gone, what would they do to achieve atonement for their sins? Up to the moment of revolt, the Temple was still the single most important symbol of their spiritual life. It was the only thing that united them as a people. When the Romans destroyed the Temple, they eliminated the only existing path to atonement. The Christian solution was to interpret Jesus' life and death in terms of an atoning sacrifice."

"Jesus died to atone for the sins of mankind."

"Now you get it! That was the innovation that transformed early Christianity. They saw in the sacrificial death of Jesus a substitute for the destroyed Temple."

Keller's gaze narrowed. "So, if the whole sacrificial atonement thing was not originally in the Torah, then the notion of killing something to atone for sin is not an integral part of ancient Judaism."

Lavi shook his head. "All of this scholarly chit-chat is very nice, but it still does not rise to the level of a motive for destroying the Shrine of the Book to cover up the stealing of the original Torah, if there even is such a thing. The Builders are fundamentalist Christians. They never cared about the Documentary Hypothesis, Darwin, the Big Bang Theory, or anything else that challenged their belief that God Himself wrote every single word."

"*S'gan Aluf*, you just found your motive. Before the discovery of the Ezra scroll, all of this Graf-Wellhaausen documentary hypothesis stuff was just an elaborate theory that only Bible scholars and their grad students could follow."

"Thank you, Rabbi Stone, for the left-handed complement." Malik said.

"All I meant, Professor, was that the entire hypothesis is built on circumstantial evidence. The evidence is overwhelming but still circumstantial. As a cop, *S'gan Aluf* Lavi, you should appreciate the difference between circumstantial evidence and a smoking gun."

"I have been known to win a case or two on both kinds of evidence."

Stone was undeterred. "I think that The Builders want to find and ultimately destroy that scroll in Shoshana bat Talmon's bone box. It is the smoking gun of Biblical history. If it exists, it will prove that Torah is a human invention. It could prove that the Documentary Hypothesis is now documentary fact. For me it's like having my own understanding vindicated."

"I would imagine there might be quite a few religious communities who would be troubled by that," Keller said.

"Religious wars have been started over much less," Lavi said.

Keller rose from the table. "How about we come back down to earth, or at least return to this century? What's our next move?"

Malik stood up, glanced at the bill for their lunch and put down cash on the table. "We need to confirm the location of the Bone Box. If it is in the museum storage facility, we need to have a plan for its rescue."

"Are we planning on stealing it, Professor?" Keller asked.

"That scroll is part of my family's heritage. I am not going to let some Bible thumpers destroy it."

CHAPTER EIGHTEEN

DATE: The Seventeenth Day of the Fourth Month, In the Seventy-first Year Since the Destruction of Jerusalem
TIME: First Hour of the Third Watch
PLACE: The House of Elias son of Yehochanan

The Guardians of the Sacred Scrolls had chosen the meeting location well. The house of Elias ben Yehochanan was ideal for a clandestine gathering, not because it sat outside of the walls of Pumbedita, but because it was surrounded by an awful stench from the four enormous clay cauldrons set against the southern wall of the courtyard. In addition to being a trained scribe, Elias was a master tanner, and the contents of these vessels were a trade secret known only to the master tanners of Bavel.

There were seventeen men and eleven women present, almost all in their late thirties, early forties. Elimelech felt out of place because of his age. He was the second oldest person in the room. Meremot was the oldest. Elimelech would have been more relaxed attending gatherings of the river traders.

Meremot began the session. For the next hour it was worship and not politics that engaged them. The rhythmic droning of the participants nearly put Yeshai into a trance. Suddenly, he realized that he was very familiar with the contents of their prayers. They were reciting lines and whole paragraphs from the Sacred Scrolls in Hebrew—from memory.

Yeshai pondered the significance of the gathering when everyone around him stood up and turned toward the western wall of the room. Meremot had walked to a wooden cabinet.

The droning changed to a more musical mode as Meremot opened the cabinet doors. The interior of the box was plain, without adornment of any kind. A jumble of parchment scrolls stood leaning against the rear wall of the box. Although Yeshai could not count the scrolls, he was sure that there were twelve of them. These were the twelve scrolls of the exile in Bavel. Were they copies or were they the originals?

Meremot removed one of the scrolls and closed the cabinet doors. He walked slowly to the center of the square and placed it gently on a table. He untied the thin leather strap that was holding the scroll together and slowly unrolled the parchment. Two men arose and went to either side of Meremot and held the edges of the scroll down by placing the end of their sleeves on the scroll. Their hands did not make contact with the parchment.

Meremot read the text in a kind of chant. Yeshai found this strange. In Samaria it was the custom to chant from the sacred scrolls only those passages that were written in the form of songs. The rest of the text was read, not chanted. Here everything was being chanted. The style was new to Yeshai's ears, but he found it very pleasant. Meremot was skilled and had a fine singing voice. Yeshai was feeling guilty about his cold treatment of Meremot when they first met. He would have to offer his apology.

The passage Meremot chanted was the story of Jacob's son, Joseph, in an Egyptian prison. Yeshai knew it well. As soon as the story concluded, the person standing to Meremot's right began reciting the very same story in Aramaic. Yeshai's Aramaic skills were not perfect, so he had a difficult time understanding every nuance of meaning. Why were there so many outbursts of laughter? It did not sound like a word for word translation. Yeshai believed that the Aramaic storyteller was adding a few embellishments of his own. When the readings had concluded, the entire gathering stood as the scroll was returned to the cabinet.

"Scribes of Judah, let our decisions be guided by the God who stood with Joseph in an Egyptian prison." The speaker was the tanner, Elias ben Yehochanan. He stood at the reading table and made a sharp noise with a small clay lamp against the wooden tabletop.

"We are joined today by a brother scribe of Judah, more recently of Samaria. I speak of Yeshai ben Gilad ben of Eliezer ben Achituv of Gezer. He is Hilkiah's cousin and the current guardian of the twelve scrolls of the Sacred House preserved among the Judean exiles in Samaria."

Yeshai stood and surveyed the room. "With the utmost respect, Elias ben Yehochanan, Please permit me to correct your statement. I would have been the guardian of the Sacred Scrolls upon the death of my grandfather and father, but the scrolls were seized by the Samaritan priests long before I became the chief priest among the Judeans in Samaria. I believe that they have destroyed them."

Whatever decorum existed in that gathering now dissolved into a deluge of angry questions. Elias was banging the clay lamp so hard it shattered and the shards flew across the room. The explosion of clay fragments caused a moment of silence. It was just enough time for Elias to shout everyone back down into their seats.

"Now would be a good time to let Yeshai ben Gilad explain his statement. If you, please..." He gestured to Yeshai to come forward.

For the next hour, Yeshai told the gathering the entire story of the twelve sacred scrolls that were protected by his grandfather and father before him, during their exile in the territory of Samaria. He revealed the existence of the Hidden Scroll and assured them that it was in a safe place, for now. He did not tell the gathering about the copy of the Hidden Scroll in his grandmother's bone box. He trusted the members of the gathering, but he could not deny the possibility that his every word was being heard by the clan of Ezekiel. If they learned about the existence of this scroll, they would stop at nothing to destroy it.

Bani ben Kadmiel, a rotund scribe who earned his daily bread by baking bread, rose to speak. "I still do not understand how anyone, let alone a priestly scribe and guardian of the sacred scrolls, could allow the scrolls to be seized? Did you not realize that they were the last remaining connection to the Sacred House of Solomon? These scrolls are important reminders of who we are. Bringing all twenty-four of them together again in Jerusalem would have been a powerful moment in the restoration of the Sacred House and the people of Israel."

Murmurs of agreement followed his challenge.

Yeshai's voice carried over the din of the angry comments being directed at him. "My brothers and sisters, from the moment my eyes encountered the Hidden Scroll, I began a routine of reading from it every day. I committed its contents to memory. After six months of daily readings, I came to understand my grandfather's purpose in assembling that scroll. Each of you is very familiar with the contents of the twelve scrolls preserved here in Bavel. Tell me, which tribes are represented in the scrolls?"

"Are you testing us?" Elias asked. "What do you mean 'represented' in the scrolls?"

"When you read the scrolls, what tribes are named?" Yeshai asked.

"The tribes of Judah and Benjamin, of course!" Bani answered.

"You say 'of course' like that is the way things are supposed to be. But my grandfather saw a great danger in the constant mention of Judah and Benjamin in the sacred scrolls."

"The other tribes, those who parted from us after the death of Solomon, are cursed." Meremot said. "It is not for us to mention them or speak of them."

Yeshai smiled and nodded. "Eliezer knew the tradition of scorn. He understood the hostility towards the vanished tribes of the Northern Kingdom of Israel. He understood that to pronounce their names would be like lifting a divine curse from their shameful exile. He also understood that for Judah to have any hope at redemption it would be necessary to bring the ten tribes of Israel back into the covenant with the God of Abraham, Isaac, and Jacob."

Meremot shook his head. "How can you bring back a people that has vanished from the earth? There are no Israelite exiles in Persia or anywhere else."

"When my grandfather faithfully assembled the texts of the twelve scrolls into the Hidden Scroll, he left nothing out. But as I read each column carefully and compared it to the original sacred text, I discovered that he did add some text. He added explanations for words or ideas that might not be understood today."

Elias was outraged. "Sacred texts cannot be altered or revised. It is like putting yourself in the position of the Almighty. Your grandfather has committed a grave sin against the God of our ancestors."

"If he is guilty of any sin against the God of our ancestors it might be his other additions. He expanded the story to include mentioning by name the tribes of the North. Those statements did nothing to change the story or any outcomes for good or for evil purposes. All his life he feared that, should the God of Abraham redeem Judah from exile, Judah redeemed could not stand alone, even with Benjamin at his side. He believed that just as not all Judeans were taken into exile in Bavel, so too, not all Israelites from the ten Northern tribes were captured by Asshur. Through the Hidden Scroll he was issuing a call to all Israelites, all descendants of Jacob, to rally to Jerusalem and the house of David and Solomon."

Elimelech stood to support Yeshai. "This would even be in agreement with the visions of Ezekiel ben Buzzi. While alive, he always spoke of the whole nation of Israel coming from the four directions and gathering together in Judah."

"How do we know that Yeshai's grandfather was not inspired by the God of our ancestors? If it is true that Eliezer left nothing of the twelve scrolls out of the single Hidden Scroll, then I for one wish to examine this scroll for myself, before passing final judgement," Meremot said.

"I too wish to study the scroll of Eliezer." Bani stood, his gaze focused on Yeshai.

A handful of others, including Ruth, stood and spoke of their desire to read the scroll.

"Do you all realize that this cannot happen overnight? said Yeshai.

Meremot stood and addressed the group. "Then first thing we must do is make sure that there are enough faithful copies of the Hidden Scroll for all who wish to read it. Yeshai, you had better be the one to make the first copy and keep it in your dwelling. When it is finished, bring the original Hidden Scroll to me. I shall make a copy of it and pass the original to Elias. From there, Elias will make a copy of the original and pass it on to Bani and so forth, until all who wish to read it have an opportunity to do so."

"This is a major undertaking. What do we do about the clan of Ezekiel while all of this copying is taking place?" Yeshai asked.

"We tell them nothing and we show them nothing," Elias said.

"You realize that we could all be charged with blasphemy, especially those who actively made copies?" Yeshai said. "Your lives might be at risk over what you decide to do."

"If the Hidden Scroll is faithful to the contents of the twelve sacred scrolls, what could be blasphemous about it?" Bani asked.

Yeshai stood to respond. "It is not the twelve sacred scrolls I am worried about. You are all well aware of another scroll presented to the people as if it were the thirteenth sacred scroll. The clan of Ezekiel might be upset when they find out that there is no mention of the *Mishkan* in the Hidden Scroll. My grandfather never saw the *Mishkan* scroll. He only knew that it was the reason for the death of his beloved twin brother. For Eliezer to even consider its inclusion in the Hidden Scroll would have been a real case of blasphemy."

"Could we stop referring to Eliezer's scroll as the Hidden Scroll?" Meremot asked.

"What would you call it?" Elias asked.

"Let's call it what it is, The Scroll of the Teaching of Moses-*sefer torat Moshe*." Elimelech knew that was the way that Gilad, father of Yeshai, referred to the hidden scroll in his letters to Hilkiah. How appropriate.

"*Sefer Torat Moshe* it shall be."

On the way back home, Ruth, Elimelech, and Yeshai said very little about the Sacred Scroll discussion. They sensed that it would be only a matter of time before the entire community knew every detail about the Guardians and their plans. No one they knew was very good at keeping secrets. This gave them grave concern.

And yet the Guardians' decision to copy and distribute the *Sefer Torat Moshe* did lift a great weight from Yeshai's shoulders. In a few weeks' time there would be multiple copies of the scroll and those would be even more difficult for Ezekiel's followers to seize and suppress. But, until he began that work and finished his first copy, he would continue to keep the precious scroll in the hiding place he created among the mud bricks forming the parapet on Elimelech's roof.

With so many troubling thoughts swirling in his mind, Yeshai was unable to find sleep. He gave up and sought the cool evening air on the roof. Gazing at the myriad stars in the heavens had a way of calming him. He walked to the corner of the roof and lifted the cover on the water barrel to raise the ladle to his lips. Suddenly, he heard the distinct sound of footsteps in the courtyard below. Yeshai reached for the sash around his waist and unsheathed the bronze dagger he carried there.

Shouts, cries, and sounds of hand-to-hand combat, boiled up from the courtyard. In less than a minute, whatever had taken place down there was over. But who won? With caution, Yeshai walked step by step down the stairway. The courtyard was pitch black.

"Who's there? Identify yourself! Why have you broken into our home?"

A flame was struck, and a torch ignited. When Yeshai's eyes adjusted to the light, he could not believe what he was seeing. Ruth and Elimelech were standing on the paving stones of the courtyard, with their hands bound by stout rope. Standing behind them were two Levites wearing the tunics and cloaks of the Jerusalem Temple cohort. Each held a bronze dagger at the throat of their captive. Tears were streaming down Ruth's face and Elimelech was struggling to loosen his bonds. Fear was in their eyes.

"Drop the knife and come over to me slowly. If you make any effort to free these people, their throats will be slashed, and they will die on the spot." In the dim light, Yeshai recognized the speaker. It was Dov ben Asher, the captain of the High Priest's guard in Jerusalem.

"What do you want? You have no authority here!"

"Surrender the scroll you call *Sefer Torat Moshe* to us, and no one will be harmed."

"Does that mean you will not attempt to return me to Jerusalem?"

"That I cannot promise."

"How dare you threaten my family with murder for a piece of parchment?"

"The High Priest has given me my orders. Give me the scroll now, or you will all die."

Yeshai resolved not to let Ruth or Elimelech be killed. He lowered the dagger to the ground. "Do not harm them. I will show you where the scroll is secured."

"Just bring the scroll to me or you will all die."

As he turned toward the stairway that led to the roof, Yeshai heard a choking-gurgling sound coming from the direction of Ruth and Elimelech. He turned to look back, fearing the worst. In the constantly changing shadows cast by the flames of the torch, Yeshai saw all three of the Levites bleeding profusely with arrows protruding from their throats. They collapsed were they stood, pools of dark red blood beneath them.

Yeshai looked in the direction from whence the arrows must have come. A squad of Persian soldiers bearing battle bows stood at the ready waiting for the order to fire. Another soldier carried a torch. Behind them was the *Pecha*, Memukan.

Yeshai spoke. "My lord, what is going on here?"

Memukan spoke in Persian. "I believe these three travelers from Jerusalem came to steal something and take you as their prisoner."

Yeshai continued in Aramaic. "But how did you know they were here?"

"My men have been following them ever since they arrived in Pumbedita. They were asking all sorts of questions about Judean scribes and the House of Hilkiah and the Sacred Scrolls. They are the ones who followed us from Jerusalem."

The Persian soldiers dragged the three corpses by their feet to the outside of the compound then threw them into an open wagon.

Yeshai extended his hand to Memukan. "Once again you have saved my family and me. How can I ever repay you?"

Memukan laughed. "Just keep your distance from Judeans traveling from Jerusalem. They do not like you very much."

"Indeed."

CHAPTER NINETEEN

DATE: March 20, 2009
TIME: 3:45 P.M. Israel Time
PLACE: Police HQ, Tel Aviv

"Why can't we just call the museum authorities and explain what's going on?" Keller asked. "They might help us locate the box."

Malik laughed at Keller. "Museum authorities, hah! Mamzers! I know those *bastards*. They will spend three weeks convening meetings of the Museum Governing Board. Then they will conduct a hearing, at which we will be called to present our evidence that the bone box is even in their collection, and if it is, that it contains the original Torah scroll. The Ministry of Antiquities' representatives to the Governing Board will immediately call the media. They cannot pass up an opportunity to campaign for more funding. They follow a simple formula. If you find something, if you find anything, ask for more funding. Representatives from the Ministry of Religion also sit on that board. They will call their rabbis and leak to them the news of the potential discovery of an original Torah. After putting all of us in *cherem*, a state like excommunication, and saying *Kaddish*, the rabbis will reach out to The Builders, inviting them to destroy the scroll. The Builders will happily oblige and then use their involvement to raise funds among their faithful."

"Tell us how you really feel about the museum authorities," said Keller.

At the entrance to Police HQ, Lavi held up his security access card and held the door open for his co-conspirators. "The Builders will need to break into the museum storage facility. We just need to catch them in the act. Then we take possession of the scroll."

They entered Lavi's office and took seats around his desk. Lavi looked out of his office window to the small park across the street. "This will not be an easy operation. First, we need to make sure that the bone box is in the possession of the museum and second, we need to find a way to gain access to its location without setting off any alarms."

Malik nodded. "In that case, I need to chat up a former friend and call in some favors. We need to be prepared for anything."

Keller rose from his seat. "We need to do some tactical planning."

"The Sergeant is absolutely correct. It is time to get down to business."

Lavi moved them into a small conference room adjacent to his office. The south end of the room had a white board. Stone and Keller began writing questions on the board in blue ink. If they had an answer, it was written in red. Malik studied the questions on the board and then crossed to the other side of the room and took possession of the only land-line phone in the room.

Stone walked away from the white board to be near Malik. "Who are you calling?"

As Malik waited for the call to connect, he placed his hand over the phone. "This is going to be a tough one. I am calling Professor Michal Levski at the museum."

"Will she know the location of the bone box?" Stone asked.

Before Malik could answer he turned his attention to the phone and started speaking. "Yes, I'll hold."

Lavi walked over and pulled Stone aside. "Professor Levski is brilliant, beautiful, and She is the curator of Balkan Jewish History at the museum. She is also Malik's ex-daughter-in-law."

"And how does she figure in all of this?" Stone asked.

Lavi smiled. "At the moment, I am not quite sure what Colonel Malik has in mind."

Stone sat down at the conference room table with a puzzled look on her face. "So, what does Professor Levski have to do with the Shrine of the Book?"

Malik, still on hold, covered the receiver and explained. "Michal has security access to the entire museum collection. The only question is whether her anger at my son will prevent her from helping in the recovery of the single greatest artifact in Jewish history?" He shushed his colleagues. "It's time to find out," he whispered, pointing to the phone to indicate that she'd come on the line. "Michal, so good to hear your voice!" Convinced he could feel her anger seething through the phone, he decided to skip the small talk and get to the point. "I need your help on a matter of national security."

Though no one could hear Professor Levski's response, the look of defeat in Malik's eyes told them all they needed to know. But he was not ready to surrender. *"Sgan-Aluf* Lavi, would you please speak with my daughter-in-law?" Malik handed him the phone, a look of pleading in his eyes.

Lavi took the phone. "Michal, it's Ronnie." Covering the phone and shrugging his shoulders, Lavi explained in a whisper. "We may have gone out for drinks once or twice."

"Listen, there's no time to explain but we need your help on a matter of national importance. I need you here at Police Headquarters, today...this afternoon. It is very important!"

Michal was unmoved. "I am scheduled to lead a tour in an hour. I can't leave now."

"Cancel it and get down here. I expect you in my office at 4:00."

Michal knew that tone of voice. This was not a ploy to take her out to dinner. Now she was curious. What part of national security could require the presence of a curator of Southeastern European Jewish History?

Lavi's next call was to Rafi and Omar. Their tactical skills would be of great value.

Stone brushed up against Keller. "What have you gotten me into, Sergeant?"

Keller looked up from the legal pad on which he was writing notes and tilted his head at Stone. "I seem to recall that you were the one who insisted we needed to get an expert's opinion from your colleague. Without our little road-trip, I would be back in Fallujah training Iraqis to dodge IED's."

Stone smiled at Keller. "That is all true, but what would we have missed?"

Keller nodded his head slowly then retreated to his place at the conference table and continued to make notes.

It bothered Stone that she had so many questions and so little time to seek answers. Where did the Builders come by their desire to rebuild the Temple? The Reverends Rumsey, father and son, are not Navy Seals. Who did they hire to create the diversion at the Shrine of the Book? Who will be at the museum warehouse to steal the bone box? Who else knows about the Ezra scroll? Who else knows about the original Torah?

Stone was exhausted by the stress and the accompanying adrenaline rushes. She put her head down on the table and closed her eyes. Before she succumbed to her fatigue, her last thought was: How will good-ole-boy, Marine Sergeant Aaron Keller go over with mom and dad? He is Jewish, even if he is from South Carolina. I cannot wait to introduce him to them. She fell asleep with an enigmatic smile on her lips.

At four-twenty in the afternoon, with a dramatic flourish, Professor Levski arrived at Lavi's conference room in the Tel Aviv Police Headquarters. Her tall frame was shrouded in a billowy floral print dress that hugged her neck and descended to just above her ankles. With the right kind of wig, she could slip unnoticed in the Orthodox neighborhoods of Mea Shearim or Bnai Brak. But instead, her shiny, long flowing natural red hair declared that this was a modern woman of fashion. Beneath the billows of cloth there were hints of a figure some would call 'statuesque.' Others would find it difficult not to stare. Malik understood what his son had seen in her. He was seeing it for himself, yet again. And then there was her voice—gravel falling over a mountainside.

Michal was in a state of vehement disbelief. She ignored everyone in the room but Lavi and directed her sarcasm toward him. "You found the original Torah, yeah right. Really! I have a tunnel I want to sell you that goes from Saudi Arabia to Eilat. You can use it to suck all the oil from the Arabian Peninsula and King Fahd will never know. What is this about, really? "

Throwing caution to the wind, Malik decided to get involved in the discussion. "Michal, I realize you and I do not have a great many bonds of trust between us."

"Oh, you do, do you? Why should I listen to you, of all people?"

"I have never lied to you about anything, and I am not lying now. Do you know what a bone box is?"

"Of course I do. Ancient cultures in this region used them for the disposal of human remains. This is local archeology 101. So?"

"We believe there is a Samaritan bone box in the museum warehouse that contains the discovery of the ages. It will make the Dead Sea Scrolls seem ordinary by comparison. Here, finally, is the answer to all those attempts to delegitimize our nation by denying our very history. We believe we have discovered the one object that makes the Documentary Hypothesis fact and not theory. Without you, we will lose this original *Sefer Torah*. Without you, a group of apocalyptic Christians may even succeed in blowing up the Shrine of the Book. We must get there before them. And we do not have much time."

Michal sat down and tried to absorb all that Malik had told her. "How do you know the bone box is there?"

"We don't," Stone said. "But we did a GOOGLE search."

"Brilliant! Is this what passes for scholarly research at TAU?"

"Go easy on her, Michal. She is a Navy Chaplain, not a student of mine. Sure, we googled "bone boxes," but based on Shin Bet's surveillance of the Rumseys, we narrowed our search to the Jerusalem area. We found a short article describing an excavation about a year and a half ago in *Shomron*/Samaria, that unearthed nearly two hundred bone boxes. According to museum fundraising newsletters, all of them were brought to Jerusalem and stored in the museum warehouse. The one we are searching for must be there."

"You don't know that! You are hoping and guessing, but you don't know anything for sure."

"Enough!" Rafi swept into the room and immediately took charge. Omar was right behind him.

"So nice of you to join our party," Keller said.

"It is nice to know that the "*Shin Bet*" can be of assistance to the United States Marines," Rafi grinned. He walked to the front of the room and loaded a flash drive into the wall-mounted computer. He pulled down the keyboard and started typing. With a few keystrokes here and a password there, Rafi had loaded a Power Point presentation and dimmed the lights over the screen. He began with a grainy silent video showing eleven men seated around a table in a bar.

Omar cleared his throat. "Sorry for the quality of the video, but here we see the Rumseys at the head of the table. To their right is Professor Carlson."

"*Yimach shemo!*" Stone blurted.

"What does that mean?" Keller asked.

Malik translated. "May his name be blotted out."

Omar continued. "With the assistance of the U.S. Navy, we have been able to identify the rest of the group around the table as recently-retired Navy Seals."

Keller stood up and tried to get a closer look, but it made the definition even worse.

"Half of them have signed on with the Rumseys for their faith and the others for the money. They will be the ones at the Shrine and at the Museum."

"Lavi briefed me on the entire situation," Omar said. "I think we can be more than helpful." He pointed out several features on the screen. "Here is the target building."

"Perimeter security is provided by concealed cameras covering the entire exterior on all sides. The cameras are monitored by the museum guards seated at the main entrance to the Museum. It's not the best system. The guards are constantly being distracted by Museum visitors during business hours and are lazy about checking their screens after the museum has closed. I think you will find it interesting that our people have detected an electronic intrusion into the closed-circuit system."

"And this means what, precisely?" Michal asked.

"It means, Professor Levski, that someone has already hacked the security cameras and will probably upload a pre-recorded view of peace and tranquility," Lavi said.

"So, what will be our response?" Malik asked.

"We are not going to prevent them from entering," Rafi said. "We are going to be inside waiting for them."

"And you need me for what, exactly?" Michal asked.

"Getting inside is the easy part. We need your security pass and codes to access the Controlled Atmosphere Storage Room. That is where the ossuaries are being kept."

"Says who?"

"The museum director," Lavi said.

"You spoke with Avichai?" Michal gave Lavi a hard look.

"I spoke to him this afternoon," Malik interjected. "I simply asked if I, as a scholar, would be able to organize a private tour for my grad students to view the Samaritan ossuaries. He explained that they were not presently on display, that they are in storage to protect them from light and air. He was excited to share that the colors are still vivid, even after 2,500 years."

"And he was not the least bit suspicious of your motives?"

"He made a tour appointment for two weeks from now and promised to show me the collection himself."

"This is like a watchdog leading the criminal to the family jewels," Keller said.

Malik smiled. "I resent that comparison, Sergeant."

"Will you get us in, Michal?" Lavi asked.

"Only if you promise to support me in my old age. I'm sure to lose my pension over this."

Lavi did not respond but smiled at Michal.

Omar took over the briefing. "We have been keeping the Rumseys under close surveillance. Our sources tell us that The Builders' operatives are planning to detonate the explosives at the Shrine of the Book at 01:30 hours this morning. We need to be inside the warehouse by 1900 hours tonight."

"Why so early?" Stone asked.

"Just in case The Builders have already placed the museum complex under their own surveillance. We will enter one at a time, in street clothes, starting at 1700 and not draw any undue attention to ourselves. We will have the advantage of surprise."

"I don't know about you guys, but whenever I think I'm operating with the advantage of surprise, the surprise rises up to bite me in the ass," Keller said.

PART III: A REPORT FROM JERUSALEM

Thereupon the people of the land undermined the resolve of the people of Judah, the exiles who had returned from Bavel, and made them afraid to build. They bribed ministers in order to thwart their plans all the years of King Cyrus of Persia and until the reign of King Darius of Persia. [Ezra 4:4-5]

CHAPTER TWENTY

DATE: In the Twentieth Year of King Artaxerxes of Persia, Corresponding to the One Hundred Forty-First Year Since the Destruction of Jerusalem, (445 BCE) In the Month of Kislev, The Ninth Month, On the Twentieth Day of the Month
TIME: Second Hour of the First Watch
PLACE: The Fortress of Susa, Persia

Nehemiah ben Hakaliah paced back and forth across the spacious room. But the room was not large enough to contain his anxiety. The visitors from Judah could arrive at any time. Despite having attained the rank of Counselor to the Emperor of Persia and Manager of the Imperial Household, he never forgot that he was a fourth-generation descendant of the exiles of Judah, and he took a special interest in his Judean brethren. He knew from earlier reports that things were bad in Judah. He needed to know exactly how bad they were.

"Ahem, excuse me, my lord," Teresh, the counselor's Medean assistant, broke into Nehemiah's thoughts.

"Yes, what is it?"

"My lord counselor, your brother, Hanani has just arrived. He seeks an immediate audience with you. He says his business with you is urgent. I must also inform you that with him are several men from Judah. Shall I show them in?"

"Yes, of course, by all means!"

A few moments later Teresh reentered the chamber, pounded his staff of office twice into the floor, and announced with an important air, "Hanani ben Hakaliah and a delegation from Judah."

Six men entered. Only one was dressed in the manner of Persia. The rest wore Judean garments, threadbare from use and still covered in dust and dirt from their journey.

Hanani cleared his throat. "My lord Counselor, permit me to introduce five representatives of the people of the land of Jerusalem, judges at the gates of the city herself." Upon entering into the room, Hanani gave a formal bow before his brother.

Nehemiah, a very big man, rushed to greet Hanani and embrace him with a smothering hug. "Teresh, please leave us and close the door behind you!"

"As you command, *Adoni.*"

"Let me look at you, brother."

Hanani was six years younger than Nehemiah. His facial features favored their mother. Always thin, he now looked gaunt from his travels.

"You have survived a difficult journey. I am grateful for your service and the Emperor himself shall know of your heroism."

"Nehemiah, please do not go on with this talk of heroism. How heroic could I be with a detachment of Imperial soldiers to protect me?"

Nehemiah resumed his seat behind an enormous wood table and extended his hands in a gesture of welcome. "Please introduce your guests."

"I have the honor to present members of the People of the Land, the chosen leadership of Jerusalem: Zacur, ben Imri, Uriah ben Hakoz, Meshullam ben Berachiah, Zadok, ben Baana, and Yoiada, ben Paseach."

"Brothers, I thank you for leaving your possessions and families behind to fulfill this important mission. Please tell me everything. We are alone. You may speak freely."

Hanani looked at his delegation and then began. "As you wish, dear brother, but our news may not be to your liking. Our brothers and sisters in Judah are on the verge of total destruction. Jerusalem's walls are full of breaches and every one of the city's gates has been destroyed by fire. There is constant warfare and lawlessness throughout the region."

Nehemiah shifted his position and grabbed the arms of his chair. "What do you believe is the cause of all this violence and unrest?"

A Judean of medium build, covered in dust, stepped forward and bowed to Nehemiah. "*Adoni,* My Lord, if I may, I am Zacur ben Imri."

Nehemiah nodded. "You may speak."

"The Empire is being dangerously weakened by fierce and constant wars with the Greeks. We have witnessed every trained soldier in the Empire, including our own Levites, pressed into service and marched away."

Hanani picked up the narrative from Zacur. "Their departure for war left us undefended, and neighboring tribes took advantage of the thinning numbers of Persian troops to attack and plunder Judah, Jerusalem, and the rebuilt Sacred House. The Samaritans, the Edomites, the Moabites, the Ammonites, the Phoenicians—each tribe grabbed all the wealth it could carry from the treasury of the Sacred House and then, for good measure, held some of our people for ransom. We were forced to pay exorbitant prices to redeem our brothers and sisters from captivity."

Suddenly, remembering his manners, Nehemiah ordered his servants to bring food and drink for his guests.

The famished visitors took full advantage of the trays of fruits and breads placed before them and restored their strength before continuing their report on conditions in Judah.

"Perhaps the only good news in all of this," Hanani surmised, "is that a large number of captives taken by the Samaritans has returned home, though they are impoverished and feel guilty for having survived their captivity while other family members have not. Some of them may be able to stand guard, but most are weakened with starvation and disease. Winter rains and snows have sent the bands of Samaritans, Ammonites, and Moabites back to their lands, but there is no doubt that with the end of the spring rains, the coming of summer will see their return to finish the destruction of Judah and Jerusalem."

Nehemiah used his knife to carve a quarter of an apple and put it into his mouth. "It would seem that the Samaritans have a lot to answer for."

Uriah ben Hakoz, a small man with a pure white beard, stood and faced Nehemiah. "The Samaritans attack us for another reason, *Adoni*—jealousy. For more than nine decades the Samaritans have resented the vast support given by Persia to sustain us in our return from exile. They believe that the God of Israel had chosen them to rule in the Land of Israel. Almost daily they accuse us of disloyalty and treachery. Fortunately, in most cases, their lies fall on deaf Persian ears.

"May I add something to the conversation, *Adoni*?" Zacur ben Imri asked.

"Please do, but you will have to speak louder. I can barely hear you."

"Of course, *Adoni*. Over the past two months we have been betrayed and lied to by some of our own Judean brethren. It is difficult to trust that what we say in this chamber will not be on the streets of Susa before the day is over."

"Speak plainly, ben Imri," Hanani said.

"As you wish." Zacur faced Nehemiah directly. "The conditions in Judah are as your brother has recounted. But what he neglected to mention, and what made our journey so dangerous, is the fact that some of our brothers and sisters in Judah, the so-called people of the land, the ones who were not exiled, are urging their people to join with the Samaritans in revolt and put an end to Persian rule in the Province Beyond The Rivers."

"Zacur is telling the truth," Zadok, ben Baana said. "We are all victims of Samaritan and Judean lies. The Samaritans and their never-exiled Judean allies tried to prevent our delegation from departing for Persia. Each of us was accused of being in league with the enemies of Persia to seek its overthrow. They describe the Samaritans as our brothers. They say we are joined together under the protection of the God of Israel.

"Merchants loyal to the God of Abraham and His Sacred House have reported in detail of their visits to Samaria. These travelers witnessed descendants of Judean priests living in Samaria since the time of the exile, leading Judeans in daily worship in the abomination the Samaritans call the Sacred House on Mt. Gerizim."

The oldest member of the delegation from Judah, Meshullam ben Berachiah, took up the tale in a voice weakened by age and the difficulties of travel.

"My Lord Counselor, may I have some water? My throat is as dry as the wilderness that separates Judah from Bavel."

Nehemiah walked to a small table in the far corner of the room and poured a cup of water from a clay jug with unusual geometric designs and flowers.

"Since I am the one who encouraged the theft, I must be the one to inform Your Excellency that we removed the sacred utensils from the ruins of our Sacred House and have brought them with us to Persia." Meshullam turned his face toward the floor.

"What!" Nehemiah's face reddened. "But why would you do such a thing? The Emperor will be very angry. His great-grandfather saw to it that the sacred objects of the House in Jerusalem were returned along with the exiles. You had no right to steal them!"

"Calm yourself, brother." Hanani placed his hand lightly on Nehemiah's shoulder. "There was good reason for us to bring the sacred objects to Persia. The gold and silver, the lavers and basins and all the rest, including the lamp stand, were about to be plundered by the Samaritans and placed in their Temple on Mt. Gerizim. These worthies of Judah are true heroes, not thieves. The objects they brought from the Sacred House of Solomon shall not become the tools of Samaritan blasphemy. We brought these sacred items to Persia because only here are they safe, until such time as we are able to return them to a reborn Jerusalem."

"There is more news, my lord Counselor," Zacur said.

"Continue, then."

"The Samaritans have a *sefer*. They describe it as the Scroll of the teaching of Moses."

"There are many such scrolls with that name among the scribes. What does this particular scroll contain?"

"Mostly the well-known stories of our tradition and those of the Kingdom of Israel before its people were exiled."

"I have heard that our Judean scribes in Pumbedita also have such a scroll. What of it? Is there a problem?"

"The Samaritan scroll declares Mt. Gerizim, not Jerusalem, as God's chosen location for the Sacred House. The Samaritans are referring to the Sacred House in Jerusalem as an abomination abhorred by God. They are vowing to plow it under by this coming summer and use the ruins to pasture their goats and sheep."

"Where did this Samaritan scroll come from?"

"Many believe that it is the work of Moses son of Amram himself, but no one really knows."

"Have any of you actually seen it?"

"I have, *Adoni.*"

"And you are...?"

"I am Yoiada ben Paseach."

Hanani extended his hand in invitation to Yoiada. "Brother, Yoiada is a scribe from a priestly order."

"Tell me what you saw."

"When the Samaritans invaded Judah forty years ago, they assembled every scribe they could lay their hands on, including my father. They forced the scribes to make copies of what they called the Scroll of the Teaching of Moses. To prevent mistakes, each scribe was given three months to prepare a scroll, using the closely guarded original as the source. I was only a young boy, but I remember the armed guards standing in my father's workroom as he transcribed from the Moses scroll day and night, resting only on the Sabbath. When he finished, the guards removed the original and my father's copy. That "original" Samaritan Scroll of Moses that I saw was written on very old parchment. The text was in the language of Abraham and King David."

"Where is that scroll now?" Nehemiah asked.

"Since that time, the scroll and the copies are brought before the people in Samaria on every festival. Passages are publicly read and translated into Aramaic so that all will understand. Groups of Judeans in Judah are using this scroll to turn our people away from the Sacred House on Mt. Moriah and toward the abomination on Mt. Gerizim."

Like an erupting volcano, Nehemiah rose to his feet. "I have heard enough! Men of Judah, I thank you once again for your bravery and your service."

"Teresh!" Nehemiah shouted.

The Persian servant was very close. He was inside the room in an instant.

"Please provide my guests with lodging and food, as well as appropriate clothing for the Royal court. Let them refresh themselves and guide them around our city. Perhaps you could show them the areas where our fellow Judeans reside. Bring them back to the fortress at the end of the second watch. I intend to present them to the Emperor."

"As you command, Adoni."

"Hanani, stay here a moment. I wish to speak with you further about this matter."

"Of course, brother."

When they were alone, Nehemiah took a pair of ornately carved armchairs from against the wall and placed them facing each other at his worktable. He indicated for Hanani to sit, and he himself sat down slowly, squeezing his girth carefully between the gracefully curved arms of the chair. He looked directly into Hanani's eyes. For an instant, he was stunned into silence. It was as if he were gazing into the face of their beloved mother.

"I know what I must do, and I must be quick about it. There is no time to waste. I shall return to Jerusalem with you immediately."

"Are you sure you want to make such a journey?"

"As much as I am distressed by the conditions of Judah and Jerusalem, I am also very concerned about this so-called Scroll of Moses you speak of. Sacred traditions are powerful tools. They can motivate whole armies faster than the promise of spoil. Prepare yourself for our return to Judah. We shall leave as soon as I secure permission from the Emperor. In two weeks, we should be in Pumbedita—in Bavel."

Hanani was puzzled. "That is a bit out of the way if we are trying to return to Judah as soon as possible. Are we going to Pumbedita because a prosperous community of Judeans lives there? Are we going to seek donations from them?"

"We don't need their donations. I want you to meet a very bright friend of mine."

"What is his name? Do I know him?"

"I don't think so. I first met him five years ago on a grain purchasing mission to Bavel. You had already settled in Jerusalem. His name is Ezra ben Seriah ben Azariah ben Hilkiah, the scribe."

It took nearly two hours for couriers to shuttle notes back and forth to and from the palace, for Nehemiah to receive the required permission to enter the palace and attend the afternoon audience with the Emperor.

Since the initial successes of Cyrus almost a century earlier, the Empire had accumulated vast riches across an enormous territory. It appeared to Nehemiah as if all those riches were on display in the Palace. No matter how many times he presented himself to his ruler, he could not overcome his childish sense of wonder at it all. Precious stones, coins, metals, sculptures, carpets, wild animal skins, and fabrics of exotic origin were all in abundance. Each visit revealed something new. The sheer quantity of the spoils of empire available meant that the room was in a constant state of change.

Nehemiah was taking a chance that he would not be admitted to speak with the Emperor. He had not been summoned and Haman the Viceroy, the emperor's gate keeper, was displeased that Nehemiah made his request for permission to attend at the last minute. If the Emperor was in a decent mood, he would be heard. If not, he would have to wait a few days and try again. Knowing that he did not have the time to wait upon the whims of the Emperor, that he had to be heard today, Nehemiah whispered a short prayer. "Grant Your servant success today and dispose that man to be compassionate toward me."

"What did you say, you fat Judean pig?" Haman ben Hamadetha the Agagite, hated all Judeans, and especially Nehemiah. "In this room, it would be wise to confine your praying to the gods of Persia. From what I hear, your god is not very successful in protecting your people or your land."

There was no question in Nehemiah's mind that Teresh had already informed Haman of all the details of his morning meeting with the Judean delegation. Haman oversaw all sub-counselor appointments in the Fortress. Nehemiah just assumed that Teresh was Haman's spy. He often used that fact to his advantage, planting false information that could be turned against Haman. In this particular instance, great subterfuge was not necessary. The Emperor was already severely paranoid. He would be pre-disposed to believing that the Samaritans were plotting against him. They had been doing so from the day when Persia took control of the Province Beyond the Rivers. The real question was what could Haman do to prevent Nehemiah from getting his way with the Emperor?

As was the custom, whenever Nehemiah appeared before the Emperor, he carried a small jug and a silver wine goblet. The jug was sealed with a thick wad of bee's wax imprinted with Nehemiah's personal seal. This was to ensure that if the Emperor died of poisoning, the blame would fall immediately and directly upon Nehemiah. With his face cast toward the ground, Nehemiah offered the jug and goblet to Haman. Haman inspected the seal and the goblet then handed them back to Nehemiah, who now had permission to open the jug and pour wine for the Emperor. As he poured, taking care not to spill a single drop, he noticed that the Emperor wore a simple white linen tunic over a long-sleeved white linen robe. Both were trimmed in gold thread.

Artaxerxes was of ordinary height but exuded power and strength. His muscles were clearly defined on his exposed limbs. Battle scars were visible on his forearms. There were even a few cuts still in the process of healing. His head was cleanly shaven. Persian women would certainly describe him as handsome.

Nehemiah, for his part, had a reputation at court for being a boisterous and gregarious fellow, trading stories and making hilarious comments about this or that member of the government. He was always careful never to embarrass the subject of his wit. In fact, many of his targets felt that, if Nehemiah had chosen them for comment, their status at court was enhanced. But today, there was no sparkle to his eyes, no smile on his lips, as he offered the goblet to the Emperor.

"Nehemiah, look at me!" Artaxerxes said. "Look into my eyes."

"As you command, my Lord Emperor." He lifted his head slightly and looked directly into the eyes of the most powerful man in the world. His gaze was broken when the Emperor raised the goblet and drank from it.

"Excellent wine! Must be from the Lebanon, no? What troubles you, my friend? I miss your laughter and your stories. I could use some laughter today. Haman has just depressed me with the taxation reports from the eastern edges of the realm."

"With your permission, Majesty, may I speak freely?"

"Your majesty!" Haman interrupted. "May I respectfully suggest that we do not have time for one of Nehemiah's stories. We have much business of state to conduct."

"Of course, you may speak, my friend," the Emperor replied while glaring menacingly at Haman. The First Counselor shrank into the background behind the throne.

"May the Emperor live forever! Why should my face not look sad when Jerusalem, the city where my ancestors are buried, lies in ruins and its gates have been destroyed by fire?"

"Haman has informed me of the most recent events in the Province Beyond the Rivers. In what way could I lift the sadness from your shoulders?"

"If it pleases his majesty and if your servant has found favor in his sight, let him send me to Jerusalem in Judah so that I may rebuild it."

Haman stepped forward. "Your Majesty, these Judeans are a drain on the royal treasury as it is! We have no resources to fund a reconstruction of Jerusalem. On the orders of your fathers, they pay less in taxes than all of your other subject peoples."

"Emperor of all Persia," Nehemiah said. "A weakened and defenseless Judah is an invitation to Egypt and Samaria. Let me strengthen Judah as a bulwark against them both. This is what your fathers intended when they sent my people back to their homes in Judah."

"Your Majesty," Haman countered. "Might I point out that the Judeans have had almost one hundred years to become a bulwark against Egypt and Samaria. They spent your wealth and that of your fathers on building a temple to their god and not on the supply and training of troops. What makes you believe that they will do now what they have failed to do before?"

"The First Counselor makes a valid point, Nehemiah. How can you succeed where others have failed?"

Nehemiah had prepared for this question by trying out answers with Hanani an hour earlier.

"Your Highness, there are two reasons we will not fail. First, our people in Judah know that your fathers were delivered victories over their enemies by the God of my ancestors. In return, your fathers released my people from their exile in Bavel and returned them to their homes in Judah. I know in my heart that the people of Judah will rally to me and to you, their emperor.

"The second reason is that we have a common enemy, the Samaritans. Since the day my ancestors were taken into exile, the Samaritans have not ceased to plot the removal of whoever ruled the Province Beyond the Rivers. They know that only Judah and its people stand in the way of their alliances with Ammon and Moab, Edom and Tyre, and of course, Egypt. The end of your wars with the Greeks has meant that the soldiers of my people have returned to Judah. Once they see the destruction the Samarians have done to their homeland while they were away fighting against the Greeks, they will assist me without hesitation. They will be fighting for their own homes and lands."

"Haman, clear the hall and close the doors behind you. I wish to speak with Nehemiah, alone."

CHAPTER TWENTY-ONE

DATE: March 20-21, 2009
TIME: 19:30 P.M. - 2:30 A.M. Local Time
PLACE: Israel Museum Warehouse, Jerusalem

"Now I have seen everything," Omar said, shaking his head as he had handed Stone a Beretta nine-millimeter automatic with a tactical holster. "Even a pistol packing rabbi."

Stone expertly slid the action open and shut, confirming that there were no bullets in the chamber. "Can I test it out on your right foot?" Stone allowed herself a slight smile, then slid a fifteen-shot magazine into the handle receiver. She walked over to a loading barrel in the corner and once again jacked the action, inserting a round.

By 19:30 hours, the sixteen-person operational team, including Stone, Keller, Malik, and Michal, were inside the warehouse. Rafi divided the sixteen into three teams. The first two teams, four members each, were made up of the police and *Shin Bet* personnel respectively. The six officers of the police counter-terrorist squad took up positions closest to the two entry points in the warehouse. The six *Shin Bet* agents had hidden themselves among the steel roof trusses in the center of the warehouse. Lavi would lead the police team at the doors. Rafi and Omar joined the *Shin Bet* team in the rafters.

The "Raiders of the Lost Box," as Malik had started referring to the group, were going through their last-minute check list for foiling the "Builders" plan to seize the bone box of Shoshana bat Talmon. The team members were wearing black, from black Kevlar helmets on their heads to the black Israeli-made boots on their feet. Even Michal had suited up and was sporting a side arm.

Malik, Stone, Keller, and Michal were ordered to stay out of the way and wait until the intruders were neutralized. They placed themselves behind packing crates along the Southern wall. Everyone inside did a final equipment check before settling in to wait for The Builders. This included a radio check of their earpieces and helmet mounted microphones, making sure they were all on the same encoded frequency.

One of Lavi's counter-terrorism specialists positioned on the roof keyed his mike. "*Chevre*, our honored guests have arrived. They're now exiting the vehicle, a tan Chevy Suburban, parked at the taxi stand across from me. There are four people in all. Each one looks fit and experienced. They are moving quickly, close to the ground. No visible weapons, but two are carrying black canvas bags. They are wearing night vision goggles. We have already disabled the Suburban. They will be at your location in two minutes."

Rafi keyed his mike twice resulting in two audible clicks, the agreed upon acknowledgement signal. Scratching sounds at the Western door of the warehouse alerted the inside take-down teams that the "guests" were working the locks to gain entrance. But nothing happened. The would-be intruders did not open the door. One minute passed, then two then three.

"What are they waiting for?" Stone asked.

"They are waiting for an explosion at the Shrine of the Book. The diversion, remember?" Malik said.

"Oh, right."

Just then the steel walls of the warehouse shook. A low rumble, like distant thunder, accompanied the vibrations. Car alarms shrieked and wailed. Sirens from fire trucks and ambulances took up the chorus a few moments later. At the peak of noise from the explosion and aftershocks, the door opened and four figures in black combat gear entered the warehouse. They scanned the enormous, dark-as-night space with their night vision gear. The *Shin Bet*/Police take-down teams held their cover positions and remained invisible. Suddenly, the bright warehouse lights went on all at once, blinding the four intruders. Although Rafi had issued the same kind of optical gear to his team members, he instructed them not to put them on. He counted on the intruders wearing theirs and decided to use it to the team's advantage.

As the intruders struggled to remove their goggles and adjust to the blinding light, the team members hidden in the rafters repelled down silently on nylon ropes. They landed directly on top of the intruders. Omar and Rafi slid down the ropes and stood with weapons at the ready covering the intruders while restraints were being applied. In less than two minutes the intruders were being marched out of the warehouse and into an unmarked van .Stone was impressed by the speed of the takedown. "Shouldn't these guys be questioned now?"

"It will wait, Rabbi. We need to keep moving." Omar said.

Keller followed Omar closely. "Remind me why we have to do this like criminals?"

"The Ministry of Antiquities demanded complete plausible deniability. If something goes wrong, this is not a government operation. It also has the advantage of keeping the Ministry of Religion and the Chief Rabbinate out of our way, should we actually find what we are looking for."

"I don't think using police vans and uniformed officers provides much deniability."

"When this gets to the press, the four we just arrested and anyone else rounded up for the Shrine of the Book explosion will be blamed for the break-in and the theft of any artifacts that are missing," Lavi said.

Stone shook her head. "Does anybody know how much damage the Builders did to the Shrine of the Book?"

"None." Rafi responded. "Our plan included rounding up the bombers before they were able to plant the devices. The delay was our fault. The demolition team had to move the devices far enough away from the Shrine so as to cause little or no damage. We had to detonate them in order to catch The Builders in the act. As a precaution, earlier this evening we instructed the curators to pull all of the Shrine exhibits currently on display and put them in the security vault."

Stone sighed in relief. "*M'tsuyan*, well done!"

The "Bone Box Raiders" removed their helmets and protective gear as Lavi collected the side arms from Stone and Keller. "You won't need these now and I won't need to answer uncomfortable questions later, should pictures of you two armed to the teeth wind up on *Facebook* ."

"Michal, it's your time to shine."

The group followed Michal and Malik to the back of the warehouse. The ceiling lights revealed a stand-alone building inside the warehouse. Close to the corner of the structure was a double door nearly four meters wide. To the right of the door was a numeric keypad and small screen glowing green. Michal approached the door, entered her personal code and placed her palm on the screen. A loud click signaled that the lock had opened. Pulling the door open, everyone craned for a look inside.

"What a *chazer-stahl*!" Rafi exclaimed.

"Pigsty," Stone translated for Keller.

"I <u>know</u> what a *chazer* is. Thank you very much."

The comment was on target. The sealed room was a jumble of archeological stuff, piled haphazardly on steel shelves. Each item had a tag attached, but that was about the only sign of visible organization.

"Is there a key to locating stuff?" Keller asked Michal.

"The staff is working on it."

Malik yelled. "Over here, everyone! Look up on top."

A row of clay containers, standing side by side like cereal boxes in a supermarket, occupied the top two shelves and covered a distance almost ten meters long. Each box was approximately fifty centimeters long and 25 centimeters wide.

"There must be two hundred of them," Stone said. "This is going to take some time."

"Rabbi, you and Professor Malik need to use this." Omar was referring to a rolling steel stairway he was moving towards the shelf unit that contained the ossuaries. The top of the stairway formed a square platform big enough for two people to stand on.

"Where did you get this contraption, the local Home Depot?" Keller stationed himself at the base of the stairway, holding it steady, as first Malik and then Stone ascended. When they reached the upper platform, they put on grey cotton gloves to prevent their body oils from damaging the boxes as they handled them. Omar passed up a light stand with two bright, yellow-framed industrial flood lamps. Malik turned the lamps on and adjusted each one for maximum coverage.

"Rabbi, there is no rush. We have until the museum office opens at 8:00 a.m. We need to get this right. Let's start by having you pull the first box out of line and then rotating it around so I can check for inscriptions. We will alternate holding the boxes, so we maintain our strength."

Stone nodded. "Sounds like a plan, Professor."

The search was both tedious and fascinating. Most of the ossuaries were simple clay boxes. A few had crude drawings of plants and animals fired directly into the clay. And then there were the boxes that could only be described as works of art. Being buried under rubble for centuries had caused most of the decoration to fade. Every so often, a section or side revealed vibrant colors and talented artists. While some of the boxes were completely clean of any markings whatsoever, most had names inscribed in simple Paleo-Hebrew letters, each a few centimeters in height. Most of the lettering was in faded black ink. A few had the letters carved into them with some kind of sharp instrument.

At two hours and thirty-eight minutes into the search, Malik smiled and held out a lavishly decorated ossuary for Stone's inspection. *Shoshana bat Talmon, eshet Eliezer ben*

Achituv hacohein v'hasofer- Shoshana, daughter of Talmon, wife of Eliezer, son of Achituv the priest and scribe.

Malik carried the artifact down the steel stairway as if it was an IED and any movement would cause it to detonate. Stone stayed close by him in case of a misstep. The rest of the members of the scroll discovery team stood in silence at the base of the stairway Each had only one question on their minds: After 2,500 years, was the original *Sefer Torat Moshe* still inside the bone box.

CHAPTER TWENTY-TWO

DATE: In the Twentieth Year of King Artaxerxes of Persia, Corresponding to the One Hundred Forty-First Year Since the Destruction of Jerusalem, In the Month of Tevet, The Eleventh Month, On the Fifth Day of the Month
TIME: Second Hour of the First Watch
PLACE: Pumbedita, Bavel

His Highness, Artaxerxes, King of Kings, insisted that his minister, Nehemiah ben Hakaliah, travel to the Province Beyond the Rivers with a military caravan, as if he were the Emperor himself on a formal state visit. Spring was almost in total bloom in Pumbedita when the delegation arrived. Wondrous colors appeared from even the smallest patches of dirt on the poorest of lanes. At the entrance to the city, flower petals were strewn before the imperial visitors.

The city elders formally welcomed their visitors from the Persian capital. They knew that every gesture of their hospitality would be reported back to Susa. Nehemiah responded warmly to the welcome but took the opportunity to announce that they would be staying only long enough to resupply and hire riverboats for the next leg of the journey to Jerusalem. This news was met with mixed feelings. On the one hand, the imperial visit brought money and commerce. That was good for Pumbedita. On the other hand, Nehemiah was a trusted agent of the Emperor. What evil reports would he convey back to the capital? The elders of Pumbedita prayed that the people would behave themselves until the Imperial entourage departed.

With the formalities of welcome concluded, there was an awkward silence in front of the city meeting hall. The visitors had been invited inside to refresh themselves with food and drink, but no one seemed to know what was supposed to come next.

Nehemiah was done with pomp. "Hanani, Have you heard from Ezra? He should be here by now. I sent word to him before we left Susa that we were on our way. He needs to know that we are going to restore Jerusalem. How much time do we have before we must continue our journey?"

"Calm yourself, brother. I believe I shall be able to hire the necessary rivercraft by early this afternoon. We will start to fill them with supplies and may have them loaded and ready to go shortly after dawn tomorrow."

"We are not going to set out tomorrow. Have you lost all track of time? Shabbat begins at sunset tonight."

"I knew that; I only thought that our mission was of such importance that you would tolerate no delays."

"Let's call this a strategic delay. I need to send another message to Ezra. Give the order for our company to refresh themselves with food and rest. We shall depart by noon on the day after Shabbat. This could be the last opportunity for rest between here and Jerusalem. We will need our strength and wits about us. The land of Samaria guards the way. Even with our military escort, we will be a tempting target for the enemies of the Empire."

Before Hanani had turned to leave, a local messenger was admitted to the meeting hall by one of the Persian sentries. Bowing low, with his forehead touching the ground, the messenger extended his right hand upwards toward Nehemiah. A parchment scroll tied with a blue chord was extended towards the Emperor's Fourth Counselor.

"I have been instructed by my master to await your reply," the messenger said."

Nehemiah untied the chord and unrolled the scroll. The writing was bold and beautiful and without any signs of hesitation. There was no question as to the identity of its author for Nehemiah had received two previous letters from the hand of Ezra. Nehemiah read quickly and re-rolled the scroll, the lines in his face relaxing. "Tell your master that my brother and I are honored to accept his gracious invitation to join him and his family for Shabbat."

"His home is not far from here. I will return one hour before sunset and guide you to it."

"Then so be it. Thank you."

By the standards of Pumbedita, Ezra's home was large. It consisted of a mudbrick and plaster walled compound more than eighty cubits square. The elevation of the house afforded a nearly unobstructed view of the riverfront. A carefully watered and tended garden contained an abundance of fruits and vegetables to keep the kitchen well stocked. There was even a raised bed of decorative flowers and plants. The overall effect was to create a sense of tranquility. Nevertheless, the peaceful ambience was shattered by four young children, two boys and two girls, shouting and squealing, as they played some sort of game that involved hiding between the rows of cucumber vines and getting very dirty.

"Children! It's time to come in and get cleaned up for Shabbat--now!" The order came from a solidly built woman dressed in a roughly woven blackish brown garment that covered her from her neck to her sandaled feet. A simple cotton white headscarf kept her hair well hidden.

"I win!" announced the oldest girl.

"We didn't finish, so no one is the winner!" objected the oldest boy.

The woman realized that she was being watched by strangers. "Oh, my goodness, you are here so early, my Lord Counselor. We are preparing a proper welcome for you and your brother, but it is not ready yet."

"Do you wish us to leave and return in an hour?" Hanani asked.

"Now that would be stupid, *Adoni*. Oh dear! I did not mean that like it sounded. Please forgive me. I have forgotten my manners. I am Yocheved, wife of Ezra and mother to these wild creatures: Aryeh, Ben-ami, Galia, and Dinah. You are most welcome in our home. Please come this way, there is a washstand where you may freshen up before we gather for Shabbat. Ezra is on his way home from the Assembly House and will be here any moment."

"Dear woman, please call me Nehemiah, and my brother is called Hanani. May the coming Shabbat find you and your entire household at peace."

"*B'ruchim haba-im*, Welcome, Welcome!" Ezra appeared, rinsing then drying his hands as he spoke. "I see that I am just in time. Please follow me to our table and take a seat." Before sitting down, Ezra kissed Yocheved and each of their children in turn.

The Shabbat table was set with intricately decorated plates, each carrying a unique floral design in dark blue. In the center of the table were clay bowls of a similar design, each filled with different seasonal foods from the local market. A roast fish large enough to feed sixteen, double the number of diners at the table, held the position of honor in the center of the feast. After the Shabbat blessings were recited, the guests were encouraged to begin passing the main course around the table.

Nehemiah watched the interaction between husband and wife closely. They sat side by side opposite him and Hanani. He noted the loving and firm way they both responded to their children's demands for attention. Their home was peaceful and orderly. It was obvious to him that the scribe's family was living a comfortable life in Pumbedita. Nehemiah was beginning to feel guilty about having to take Ezra away from all of this beauty and security and plunge him into the dangers and uncertainty of restoring Jerusalem. He let out a long-sustained sigh as he realized that he had no choice. How would he break the news to Ezra and his family?

As the meal progressed, Ezra encouraged his guests to tell stories of Susa or Jerusalem. In Nehemiah's telling, Susa was a city of wonders and for Hanani, Jerusalem was a city of possibilities. The children were enthralled. They joined in a rousing *birkat hamazon* and, having finished the grace after meals, they assisted their mother in clearing away the dishes.

Much to Yocheved's surprise, Ezra could not sit still. He joined his children in clearing the table. The telling of stories of Susa and Jerusalem reminded Ezra that as pleasant as the Shabbat meal was, his honored guests were here for a purpose. He thought he might know what that purpose was, but he would have to wait until his guests were ready to reveal it. Perhaps sharing his own secret would loosen their tongues.

"After two dusty weeks on the road, this meal was like a taste of what the Persians call paradise," Hanani praised Yocheved. "Everything was delicious!"

Nehemiah, who felt as if he was enduring starvation on the journey, agreed. "I am renewed. I am revived! Thank you for this celebration."

Ezra turned to his guests. "You have honored our family by your visit. My Lords, I have something I must show you." He now spoke with a sense of urgency in his voice. "Please follow me." He led his guests up a flight of mud brick stairs to his workroom. The room was six cubits square with wide windows on three sides. Ample light was provided by a shelf filled with small oil lamps that surrounded the room on three sides. They had all been lit before sunset. A doorway on the fourth side opened onto a flat rooftop covered with straw mats. This night the distinguished guests from Susa would sleep here in the cool outdoor air, under a brilliant blanket of stars.

Now that Ezra and his guests were in his workroom, his urgent need to show his guests his work subsided. It was Shabbat, after all. Perhaps they would explain the purpose of their journey, first. Ezra was plumping up enormous pillows for the long couch that went nearly the entire length of the eastern wall of the room. Then he began filling wine cups with a sweet thick wine to make sure that his two guests were comfortable. The room was a sanctuary of quiet.

With cup in hand, Nehemiah sipped and slowly walked the perimeter of the workroom. He spoke as he walked. As if reading Ezra's mind, he decided it was time to inform

Ezra of the role he was about to play in their journey. "Do you know why we have made this side trip on our journey to Jerusalem?"

"I am thinking it may have something to do with a sacred scroll."

"How do you know that?" Who told you?" Asked Hannani.

"That is what I was anxious to show you."

Nehemiah's eyes grew large. "Do you have it here?"

Ezra nodded slowly.

Three large tables stood in the center of the room and formed a rectangle, with the fourth side open. Nine high stools with basket-weave tops were scattered around the tables. A basket sat in the center of each table, filled with potsherds, presumably to hold down rolls of parchment. Clay inkpots were stored on wooden shelves in between the windows, along with the ingredients and tools for making ink, quills, and parchment, and fine sand for drying ink on parchment.

"Please have a seat," Ezra said.

Walking to the center of the room, Ezra knelt on the floor and lifted a bright red wool rug. He inserted the tip of a scribe's knife into a notch that was all but invisible in the centermost board. Carefully he pried it upward. Beneath the board was a long, finely stitched leather drawstring bag. Ezra loosened the drawstring and withdrew a scroll that was a full cubit in length and two handbreadths thick.

"Thank you for making sure the scroll is secure," Hannani said.

Ezra smiled. "Judean lackeys from Samaria are everywhere. They have heard rumors. All they know is that we have some kind of sacred scroll. They fear what its contents may do to weaken the power of Samaria and strengthen Judean loyalties to Persia. We have worked too long and too hard on this scroll to have it taken from us now."

Ezra untied a blue chord around the scroll and unrolled it on the table. He then weighed down the corners of the exposed columns with several of the potsherds. Nehemiah took a small clay oil lamp down from a shelf and leaned in, careful not to drip olive oil onto the parchment.

"It is so beautiful. Is it the work of one scribe?" Nehemiah asked.

"Yes."

"Are you that scribe?" Hannani asked.

"I am the scribe, but I am not the sole author or editor."

"What is that supposed to mean?"

"It means, my Lord, that a group of us known to each other as the *Shomronim*, the Guardians, are responsible for this effort."

Nehemiah laughed. "Very amusing!"

"What is, my brother?" Hannani asked.

"Judean exiles in Bavel prepare a scroll to spiritually empower Judah in its battle against the Samaritans, and they call themselves *Shomronim*, the very name of the Samaritans in Hebrew. Very clever."

"My Lord, do you know the source of the deep and bitter enmity that exists now between the Judeans and the Samaritans?" Ezra asked.

Nehemiah took another sip of wine. "Probably nothing more than the endless squabbles of empire, I would imagine. Children need to be reassured, from time to time, that their father, in this case, Artaxerxes, prefers them over all others."

Hannani shook his head. "You can be so Persian sometimes, my brother,"

"Now what does that mean?"

"It means that when you have the power of the empire in your hands and at your disposal, you tend to see things only from the heights of majesty. You need to come down to ground level, our level, where the simple people live. It will give you and your Emperor some much-needed perspective."

"Excuse me, my Lords, but I have much to discuss with you and given the brevity of your sojourn among us, so little time. Perhaps I can give you that ground level perspective you seek. This scroll spread out before you is the reason for the hatred."

"You must be joking!" Nehemiah said.

Ezra raised an eyebrow. "I am deadly serious."

Barely had the words left Ezra lips when, three flaming arrows flew through the windows on the Eastern side of the workroom and struck the floor in the center. Ezra and Hanani jumped into action and using their sleeves snuffed the flames of two of the arrows. The third arrow was stuck in the red wool rug in the center of the room, setting it alight. Nehemiah doused the flames with the contents of a basket of loose sand he had located in a corner of the room.

"Is the scroll damaged?" Hannani asked.

"It was not touched. It is safe, for now," Ezra replied.

Nehemiah walked over to the eastern window and cautiously looked down into the courtyard. "Two things are now certain. First, the idea that the scroll is an important factor in Judean/Samaritan enmity, is very real."

"What is the second certainty, my brother?"

"The Samaritans know it is here."

CHAPTER TWENTY-THREE

DATE: March 22, 2009
TIME: 8:00 P.M. Local Time
PLACE: Hebrew Union College School of Biblical Archeology 13 King David Street, Jerusalem

The clean-up at the museum warehouse took nearly an hour. They wiped the place down and made sure that they left no trace of their presence. During the clean-up, the "Raiders" discussed where they could safely open and examine the contents of the box.

Michal was adamant. "We have already placed the museum in a very public spotlight. We cannot open it here. The directors will want total control, and the media will be all over us."

Malik agreed. "We need a proper antiquities lab and, if we find what we hope to find, space to hold a press conference without any bureaucratic interference."

Stone laughed. "I know just the place and they owe us, big time."

"Where is that?" Keller asked.

"The Hebrew Union College. They can make up for their esteemed faculty member's theft of the Ezra Scroll from their so-called secure vault."

"Perfect! Make the call," said Malik

Stone placed a call to the Dean of Hebrew Union College's Jerusalem campus. After apologizing for waking him up in the middle of the night, she passed her phone to Rafi, who walked to a distant corner of the warehouse and continued the conversation with the Dean. After a long ten minutes, he returned. "The Dean has agreed to allow us to use the workroom at the college."

"And that's what that whole conversation was about?" Stone asked.

"He was cautious, at first. Then I hinted that the Prime Minister would look favorably upon the College's petition for additional land for expansion as gratitude for the College's help. After he got over his shock that I was so well informed about the needs of the College, he told us to meet him in twenty minutes at the back entrance near Beit Shmuel."

The Dean escorted the team to the workroom and then departed. Michal, her task fulfilled and with the thanks of the team and a passionate kiss and promise from Lavi to call her, took a cab home to the Rechavia neighborhood. The six who remained, Omar, Rafi, Lavi, Malik, Stone and Keller were fidgeting with nervous anticipation.

The high intensity lamps over the worktable put the box in a very dramatic circle of white light. In silence the team members slowly walked around the table and simply stared at it. The only sound in the room came from the air conditioning system.

Keller could not hold back. "Excuse me for asking, but are we going to open this up now, or what?"

Malik moved next to Keller. "Sergeant, we must take our time and try to figure out how to open this box with the least amount of damage. It has been intact for two thousand five hundred years. I do not want to be the one who shatters it in one misapplied chisel blow."

"Professor, it is not necessary to hit it with a chisel. I may be a Jew boy from South Carolina, but I am very handy with all sorts of cabinetry tools. I have been building stuff with my dad since I was five. He used to tell me that Jesus was not the only carpenter in our tribe. My advice, we should use a Dremel tool to open the box."

"A what?" Malik asked.

Instead of explaining, Keller turned to the shelf behind him and lifted a fist-sized device with what looked like a small drill bit with a disk on top. The disk was a sanding tool, very sharp at its edge.

"We should use this to cut the bottom of the box all around. Then you simply lift the box, revealing its contents. Since the bottom is free of decoration you will not lose anything of historical value."

Malik furrowed his considerable eyebrows as he evaluated Keller's advice. "Not a bad idea. Does anyone have any objections?"

"We just have to make sure that nothing breaks when the box is lifted." Stone turned to Keller. "You make the cut, Sergeant. Professor, you will lift the box when the cut is complete. The rest of us will take a side and stand at the ready to prevent anything from falling out and smashing to pieces."

Keller laughed as he hefted the Dremel tool and plugged it into a socket at the side of the table. "When did you become the "AIC?""

"The what?" Malik asked.

"The Archeologist-In-Charge."

Stone's face turned crimson from embarrassment. "I'm sorry, did anyone else have a better plan?"

"It's as good a plan as we are going to come up with. Just get on with it, already." Malik said.

Keller located a pair of safety goggles on the shelf above the power tools and put them on. The rotary cutting tool was noisy and produced an enormous amount of dust. Stone anticipated the dust and provided the team members with surgical masks. Beneath the bright lighting, the dust appeared like a terra cotta fog. Stone went to the doorway and flipped a fan switch. The high-powered exhaust fan removed the visible suspended dust in less than twenty seconds.

Malik, wearing cotton gloves, grasped the box from the two narrow ends and started to lift. As he lifted, the contents began to fall out onto the table. An assortment of sepia-colored bones slowly cascaded from all sides. Omar, Rafi, Stone and Keller, made sure that nothing rolled off the table. Malik continued to lift the box from its base.

Disappointment hung in the air.

"With all due respect to Shoshana bat Talmon, is that all there is?" Omar asked.

"Something is not right," Malik announced.

Stone crossed her arms. "No kidding."

"That is not what I meant. The box is heavier on one side than the other." Malik proceeded to invert the box and set it down on a clear part of the table, but still under the lights. The reason for the uneven weight distribution in the box became immediately apparent. There was a sealed rectangular clay box within the ossuary that ran from one end to the other and was half as wide as the width of the box.

"Sergeant, you are pretty handy with that Dremel thing. Do you think you can make precise cuts along the top so we can see what is in the inner box? I don't want to put any unnecessary pressure on you, but this cut needs to be very carefully done. First, because we do not want to ruin the ossuary itself, and second, because we do not want to damage the contents of this compartment."

Keller lowered the safety goggles resting on his forehead. He studied the compartment from a number of different angles before starting to cut from the unattached corner. He continued down the long side, moving the tool very slowly.

In less than ten minutes the top was free. Malik reached in and carefully picked up the clay piece with both hands. He lifted it out of the box and lowered it slowly to the table. Everyone drew a breath. An object wrapped in leather filled the compartment. There was no thong or rope binder. The leather was exceedingly dry and brittle.

"Stand back," Stone said. With a small spray bottle, she cast a mist over the entire length of the leather object.

"What are you doing? You will ruin it!" Omar said.

"Relax! This is a weak mixture of water and mineral oil. It will moisten the leather just enough to allow us to open it up. I am not spraying anything beneath the outer layer."

Gently, Stone started to loosen the wrapping. There was some flaking of the dry leather but most of it was intact. The leather was wound around the object three times. With the wrapping now flat on the worktable, an ancient scroll was revealed.

"Professor, it's your turn," Stone said with a smile.

"I can't believe that I am so nervous. My hands are shaking!"

"You can do this, Professor," Omar said.

"Here goes." Malik inspected the parchment with a large self-illuminated magnifying glass. With only a featherweight amount of pressure, he touched the scroll with his gloved hand.

"It does not appear to be brittle. We can thank the atmospheric controls at the museum for its state of preservation. In fact, it is probable that the condition of the parchment improved since the time when the ossuary was brought to Jerusalem for storage. The moisture content of the parchment would have been gradually increased. That would have been the best way."

Keller was growing impatient. "Could you please get on with it and save the 'Ask Mr. Science' lecture for later?"

"Sergeant, I am surprised at you. This scroll has been waiting for this moment for 2,500 years. Malik took a flat, narrow spatula-like instrument and slid it under the edge of the parchment. He was making sure that there was nothing causing the outer edge to stick to the layer beneath. "So far, so good."

After thirty minutes of very careful prying, the first columns of the text were revealed. The writing was very small, Paleo-Hebrew. There were no spaces between the words.

"*B'reshit bara elohim et hashamayim v'et haaretz.*" Malik was holding a wooden stick. It was a stylus, actually. He moved it along as he attempted to read the words. His eyes were moist with tears of sheer joy.

"In beginning, God created the heavens and the earth..." Stone could not help herself. Her translation came as an involuntary reflex.

Dawn came and went. The unrolling and reading continued. Students seeking to enter the workroom for their morning classes were blocked by two Shin Bet agents in combat fatigues. Stone started to alternate with Malik in reading the text. Along the way they noted variations in the text from that of the Masoretic Hebrew text, established as the standard Torah text since the ninth century.

At 2:30 in the afternoon, they realized that the Book of Exodus was missing all references to a *Mishkan*. Malik shook his head in wonder. "This is an astonishing development. Just as some scholars had imagined over the years, the Biblical Israelites had no tradition of a tabernacle in the wilderness. This is the kind of irrefutable evidence the Builders feared most. Moveable sanctuaries were not a part of ancient Israelite religious tradition."

With pauses only for personal necessity and cold cardboard pizza, the reading finally concluded at 9:30 p.m. As the last section of parchment was unrolled, there would be yet one more surprise, perhaps the greatest of them all: Several small sheets of thin parchment tightly rolled and placed in the center of the main scroll. Even an amateur could see that the lettering on the sheets was by the same hand as the entire larger scroll. Both Malik and Stone had trouble separating the letters into words and sentences. For the main scroll there was a Biblical context to guide them. For these additional sheets there was no frame of reference. After thirty-five minutes the task became more straightforward. The smaller parchment sheets formed a letter from Eliezer ben Achituv. It told his story and that of his twin brother. Malik read the text of the letter out loud. He was especially moved by Eliezer's account of his losing control of the Sacred Scrolls to the Samaritan *cohanim* as a catalyst for writing the single *Sefer Torat Moshe*. When Malik finished deciphering the letter, no one uttered a sound. The only exceptions to absolute silence were the soft rhythmic clicks of a clock on the wall.

"Extraordinary!" Stone finally broke the tension.

Rafi was seated on a bench behind the table. His head was resting against the wall. His eyes were closed. "Now what do we do, *chevre?*"

Malik stretched his arms out to the side like a plane about to take off and moved his head in a circular motion to relieve the stiffness in his neck. "Well, I will tell you one thing we are not going to do," Malik said.

"What's that?" Stone asked.

"We are not going to ship this off to some lazy-ass philologists who will parse this discovery into a million bits of disconnected information and publish two lines a year in a journal so obscure not even Google can find it."

Keller smiled. "Gee, professor, tell us how you really feel."

"I am as serious as I have ever been in this matter. We are going to publish our findings tonight!"

Stone was appalled. "Oh please, you cannot mean that. We have not slept for two days. We cannot even see straight. I don't even know to what journal to submit the publication."

"We are not using a journal. We are not going to print our findings. We are going to use CNN, SKYNEWS, *Al Jazeera*--OK, maybe not *Al Jazeera*."

"*Sgan Aluf* Lavi, call your public information officer and tell him or her we have an amazing discovery to announce!"

"Should I describe the nature of the discovery?"

"Tell the officer anything that will get all the networks here in two hours."

"Why two hours? It will be midnight!" Stone was still not convinced of Malik's plan.

"That's right. That gives each of us enough time to grab a shower and some fresh clothes. We'll head to the dorm in Beit Shmuel one at a time. We are not letting this discovery out of our sight, not even for an instant. By having the cameras and reporters here, we will reduce the likelihood of some fanatic or other trying to steal or destroy the scroll."

CHAPTER TWENTY-FOUR

DATE: In the Twentieth Year of King Artaxerxes of Persia, Corresponding to the One Hundred Forty-First Year Since the Destruction of Jerusalem, in the Month of Tevet, the Eleventh Month, On the Fifth Day of the Month
TIME: Second Hour of the First Watch
PLACE: Pumbedita, Bavel

Ezra and his guests were angered by the brazen attack. Nehemiah descended the stairway and sought out the Persian soldiers assigned to guard them. They were nowhere to be found. Ezra returned the scroll to its hiding place in the floor. Hannani was collecting the sand off the floor with a small broom. He then examined the arrows carefully. They were not of Persian origin. Nehemiah returned to the workroom but was too agitated to sit down. He started to pace around the room, again.

"You already knew this struggle was about sacred scrolls," Ezra stated as fact. "You would not be in my home if you did not know this to be true. So, what do you want from me?"

"It **is** all about scrolls, sacred and profane, Ezra. You are correct. We know that the Samaritans are in possession of a scroll they called the *Sefer Torat Moshe*. They parade it about and teach from it. We know that their Scroll of the Teaching of Moses declares Mount Gerizim in Samaria as God's chosen site for the Sacred House, not Jerusalem. We need to counter that scroll with one of our own, a scroll the long-suffering exiles of Judah can rally around, a scroll that truly comes from the scribes of the Sacred House of Solomon. We believe the scroll beneath your floor is that scroll. Where did it come from? Did you and your fellow scribes copy this scroll from the one Yeshai ben Gilad ben Eliezer brought with him during his escape from Judah?"

"Yes, it is a copy of Yeshai's scroll, but there have been additions." Ezra removed the scroll from its hiding place and held it carefully in his arms. He had come to the conclusion it was time for the scroll to be made public.

"What additions?" Hannani asked.

"This scroll is Yeshai's scroll combined with the *Mishkan* scroll."

"Isn't that the forgery made up by Ezekiel ben Buzzi? It was all about the construction of a sanctuary in the wilderness, after the Israelites left Egypt."

"You are well informed, Hannani," Ezra exclaimed. The scribe continued. "Our Guardian scribes agonized over whether or not to include it in this particular scroll of Moses. Caution prevailed. We all felt that we must have the support of the Judean priests. They are more likely to proclaim the authority of this version of the scroll of Moses if the *Mishkan* scroll is included.

"My fellow Guardians and I agree that this scroll could be the banner that will bring Judah together. Why not take it with you now, while you have a military escort? I present it to you and the people of Judah in Jerusalem. Guard it well. May it keep you safe on your long journey." Ezra bowed his head and held the rolled scroll across his outstretched hands toward Nehemiah.

"Return it to its hiding place," Nehemiah countered. "I will see to it that you have trustworthy guards to protect your home and family. We dare not take it with us now. Too many enemies are interested in the failure of our mission to Jerusalem. Besides, Jerusalem is not yet secure in Persian hands. There is much work to be done in rebuilding the city, its walls and gates. I will send word to you when it is time for you and your fellow priests to join us. Then, together we shall present the *Sefer Torat Moshe* to the people in a grand public ceremony."

"I shall do as you ask, My Lord."

The last of the oil lamps in the workroom sparked and guttered. In near total darkness and complete silence, the three men made their way to the rooftop door and walked out onto the sleeping space. All three looked up at the stars in the sky. It was then that Nehemiah recalled an oft-told tale about the grandfather of Israel. As he remembered the exact words of God's promise to Abraham, a smile crossed his lips. *"I will make your offspring as numerous as the stars in the sky."*

Ezra stared out of the window.

"Are our guests comfortable on the roof?" Asked Yocheved.

"It's a beautiful night. They will be fine."

"Come to bed. We have had enough excitement for one evening. Are you worried about another attack?"

"Thanks to our guests, the house is surrounded with soldiers."

Yocheved spoke in a whisper. "Did you give Eliezer's psalm to Nehemiah?"

"No. I never told him about it."

Yocheved sat upright. "Why not?"

"Because he does not need to know of that scroll. Right now we need to put our trust in the scroll that the Guardians have prepared. There must be only one *Sefer Torat Moshe*. If the psalm falls into the hands of the Samaritans, they might learn the location of Eliezer's other scroll and destroy it."

"What if Nehemiah loses the torah scroll you gave him?"

"He did not take it. He asked me to hold onto it until he sends word for me to join him in Jerusalem."

"Ok, but what if you lose the scroll and are killed in the process?"

"Thank you for your good wishes. I know this sounds crazy, but Eliezer's psalm will be a surety that someone will be able to locate the second scroll and restore that one to our people."

"My dear husband, it is crazy! Who will that someone be?"

"It will be a member of our family."

"And how do you know this?"

"Because every descendant of Eli and Zadok will be taught by us. They will know of the existence of the psalm. It will become a part of our family's history. I shall hide the psalm by placing it among the other discarded sacred scrolls in the storeroom of our house of assembly."

"Do you think that is wise?"

"As long as it is among other sacred texts it will be secure. Unless the seeker knows what to look for, it will be like looking for an oak sapling in a forest. The Holy One will decide when the time is right for it to be discovered."

CHAPTER TWENTY-FIVE

DATE: March 22, 2009
TIME: 12:30 A.M. Local Time
PLACE: Hebrew Union College School of Biblical Archeology, 13 King David Street, Jerusalem

Stone and Keller stood at the top floor window and gazed out at the chaotic scene below.

The networks started showing up just after 11:00 p.m. and King David Street was bumper to bumper with satellite transmission trucks from Mammilla street to just past the King David Hotel. Under klieg lights, a gaggle of reporters were doing stand-up introductions in front of the main gate to Hebrew Union College. They were describing the information they had been given so far and then filled time with factless speculation.

Stone turned to Keller and spoke, as if breaking a spell. "Now what happens to us?"

"Well, ma'am, how about I go back to saluting you and you save my ass from a court martial?"

"That is not what I meant, and you know it!"

"How's about I file a petition with my CO for permission to marry a superior officer?" Stone caught her breath as Keller continued to ramble on.

"I am truly having a problem with one aspect of our relationship. I do not know which is going to give our married life more problems: the fact that you outrank me or the fact that you are my rabbi." Keller pulled Stone away from the window and enveloped her in a firm embrace.

"Please excuse us, but the Dean has just opened the gates, and the press is descending upon us," Rafi said, interrupting their kiss.

It took several elevator trips for the assembled members of the press to reach the workroom. There wasn't a spare centimeter of space left. The Dean insisted that, as the CEO of the Jerusalem campus, it was his duty to welcome the press and introduce Professor

Malik. The Ezra Scroll Team, as they started to style themselves, agreed that Professor Malik should make an opening statement detailing what was found, then introduce the team members and describe their individual contribution to the discovery.

At the insistence of Lavi, Rafi, and Omar, Malik left out the juicy parts about trucks ramming cars on the Jerusalem highway, bombs destroying tea shops, and the involvement of the Samaritan community in general.

Malik helped the press to connect the Ezra Scroll discovery to the break-in at the Shrine of the Book and the Israel Museum warehouse. That morning the press had already been given information that characterized The Builders as a Christian Fundamentalist terror organization bent on the destruction of the Dead Sea Scrolls and anything else that challenged their radical understanding of Scripture. The media were even given the video to prove it. A general Interpol warrant was sworn out for the location and apprehension of the Builders leadership, the father-and-son Rumsey duo.

A very attractive female reporter from SKYNEWS posed the first question with plenty of attitude. "How do you know that this scroll is not just some well-orchestrated hoax? We have had these sensational announcements before, you know."

"Christine, the scroll will have to be subjected to the usual testing and analysis to confirm the date of the materials used, but the discovery of the scroll came as a result of an ancient, coded message discovered two weeks ago, hundreds of miles away."

"Where, Professor?"

"I am not at liberty to tell you that, right now. To do so would jeopardize even more unprecedented discoveries. I am hopeful that there will soon come a time when we can reveal the reasons for our lack of candor on this matter. "Next question. You." Malik was pointing at the chief of NBC's Middle East Bureau.

"You were vague about the role of the rabbi and Mr. Berg in this matter. Are you hiding something?"

The team agreed that revealing the identities of Stone and Keller would allow a connection to be made quickly to Keller's posting in Fallujah. The two of them were wearing simple yet effective disguises--a blonde streaked wig for Stone, a shaggy layered wig and bushy mustache for Keller.

"They were instrumental in bringing the coded message to my attention."

"And that's it?"

"That's it. You in the second row, what is your question?" Malik indicated a reporter for the Israel daily newspaper, *Haaretz*. He was also a stringer for the *New York Times*.

"In your professional scholarly opinion, what is the significance of this discovery?"

"Since the days of Spinoza in the Seventeenth Century, scholars have theorized about the probability of multiple authors of the Torah. We call this the Documentary Hypothesis. A central element of that hypothesis is the assumption that some individual or group was responsible for arranging and editing a number of distinct texts into the document we refer to as the Torah. Until today we did not know the actual Who or the How. Now we know."

"Aren't you concerned that this would do great damage to people's faith in the divine origin of the scriptures?"

"Look, since the nineteenth century millions of followers of non-orthodox religious traditions have taught and still teach that the Hebrew Scriptures represent a human document describing how ordinary humans related to God in a particular place and at a particular time in history. Our discovery helps us move from theory to fact. One commentator described the Hebrew Scriptures as a library. I look at the matter in this way. Today we have been able to reveal the identity of the librarian and his descendants. The literature is still magnificent, compelling, passionate, and insightful. That will never change."

April 9, 2009 4:30 P.M
On the Tel Aviv Beach Behind a Shin Bet Safehouse

Following the public announcement of the discovery of the *Ezra Scroll*, Professor Malik saw to it that Stone and Keller would not be disturbed or hounded by the international media. Since the U.S. Navy was generous enough to provide them both a thirty-day leave, Malik arranged for their accommodations in a *Shin Bet* safe house that masqueraded as a shabby beach-front hotel. It was right on the Tel Aviv Promenade, and the penthouse suite they occupied was anything but shabby. They did not waste their time speculating about who had occupied the suite before them. They decided to stay under the covers except for meals. On the best weather-days, just before sunset, they went down to the beach for a swim. As the sky glowed with an amazing array of pastel reds and oranges, they would sit holding hands and gaze towards the west. On their last night at the beach, their conversation took a very emotional turn.

A dark cloud had passed across the sun, which was setting before them. The temperature dropped and the wind suddenly picked up loose sand and spun together a three-meter-tall dust devil. Aaron placed a sweatshirt around Abby's shoulders and gave them a light squeeze.

"Should we walk back? Is it getting too cold for you?"

"Can't we just stay here forever?"

"Wouldn't that be breaking the rules?"

"That's a hoot. You never follow the rules."

"If I followed the rules and played it safe, we never would have met. Look, all good things must come to an end."

She punched him on his upper arm with force. "I do not want this to end!" she said with surprising vehemence.

"Abby, what's going on?"

"Aaron, I love you!"

"I love you too, ma'am."

She punched him again, harder. Since Aaron was a true buff Marine, her fist just bounced off of him.

"You don't get it, do you? I've fallen in love with a grunt Marine--a Jewish grunt Marine, but still a Marine. I've slept and screwed my way into numbness with an enlisted military policeman, a man who has no future, no prospects, no marketable skills."

"What do you mean, 'no marketable skills'? I am a military cop with a spotless record. I am a trained killer. I speak a little Arabic. I could get paid ten times what I am getting now doing the same kind of work for one of those private security companies. I do have a future! I could get a job with almost any police department in the States. I could work for Homeland Security. I do have prospects, Raaaabbi Stone! They may not be the kind of prospects that would impress your parents, but they are honorable and not all that bad."

"Do any of those prospects involve a life where you are not subject to getting your head blown off by snipers or losing the lower half of your body to IED's, or getting killed in a drug bust in a dark alley in Charleston?"

Abby burst into tears. Aaron tried to comfort her, but she broke free from his embrace and started walking away from the water's edge, toward the stairway leading off the beach and back to their hotel. He caught up with her and folded her into his arms and held on tightly.

"Listen to me! I understand. I do not want to lose you either! But you need to know that I truly love you and will do whatever it takes to spend the rest of my life with you."

An hour and a half later, Abby and Aaron were in the hotel's private dining room among their *Ezra Scroll* teammates, paying virtually no attention to any of them. The silence between them was like a heavy curtain, allowing each to be in their own little world. The Israeli government was the host for this intimate party and no limits were placed on what they could order off the menu. Hiding behind the leather-bound covers of the wine list, Aaron tried to ask their server questions that would not give him away as a complete wine ignoramus. The server found it impossible to hide his grin. Eventually, Aaron retreated to the price side of the list and chose the most expensive red he could find. When the server poured, they lifted their glasses and clinked them together and it was the first sound that they shared since they left the beach.

After a few sips, the rich red wine helped to part the curtain of silence. Abby began the conversation with a dainty clearing of her throat.

"Aaron, I am so sorry."

"For what? You've nothing to be sorry about. We are both old enough to want to make the right decisions for the rest of our lives. God knows, I have made enough of the wrong ones. I have never felt so sure about anything until now. But stress is a terrible thing. Adrenaline rushes will mess with your mind."

"What in the world are you talking about? Who said anything about adrenaline?"

"The whole business with the *Ezra Scroll* and the original Torah was pretty intense. This little R and R was a good way to deal with that intensity. But the rush does wear off and the depression sets in."

"I am not...depressed!"

"That's not what I am talking about."

"So, what then?"

"You are so beautiful and so special; I want to get this right. I want a completely clear head, and I want you to respond to me with an equally clear head."

"And the wine is supposed to help with that?"

"I have had exactly two small sips for courage."

"You're a grunt Marine. How much more courage do you need and for what?"

Aaron raised his white cloth napkin and threw it down on the table with a bit of a flourish. Their server came over and without a word placed a small black box on the plate in front of Abby. Aaron dropped to one knee, grasped Abby's hands in his and looked directly into her dark eyes. "Lieutenant Stone, will you marry me?"

"Wh..wh..how in the hell did you pull this off? You've been by my side since the morning we arrived in Tel Aviv."

"Are you going to interrogate me or answer my question?"

My answer is yes!" Abby stood up and pulled Aaron to his feet and they embraced and kissed to the vigorous and sustained applause of the *Ezra Scroll* team members.

"Mazal Tov! It's about time, you two."

"Professor Malik?" Abby was dumbfounded. "We didn't think you were going to make the party."

"I don't know how much longer I could have remained hidden in that freezing wine room." The professor was holding a champagne bottle in one hand and two fluted glasses in the other.

Abby turned to Aaron, her voice rising in intensity. "How did you ...you planned this in advance? Did you plan our argument on the beach too?"

"The argument was completely spontaneous, and mostly your fault," Aaron teased. "In answer to your second question, I had a long conversation with our dear professor before we settled into our room here. He assured me that he was familiar with the finest diamond merchants in Tel Aviv."

Abby hugged the professor and gave him a big kiss on his cheek.

Malik fumbled with the foil wrapping on the champagne bottle, ready to wrestle with an oversized cork, only to find a twist cap.

"My apologies, children. This was the only champagne in this establishment, *Chateau Lefitte Bupkes* or something equally mundane. It will have to do. First a toast to the newly engaged couple, then I have some interesting news I need to share with you." Malik poured the champagne then emptied the bottle by offering its contents to the rest of the celebrants in the dining room.

"To the couple who discovered a priceless treasure...each other! *L'chaim!*"

As things began to settle down, Malik gestured for Abby and Aaron to be seated. He pulled up a chair from an empty table nearby, hunched forward and motioned with his hands for the couple to lean in. Malik stole a glance at the tables around them, satisfying himself that they would not be over-heard.

"What are you concerned about?" Keller asked. "Everyone in this room has a high Israeli or American security clearance—including the servers."

"Just as we feared, our friend has gone to Iraq. He is asking a lot of questions about a particular neighborhood and a firefight that took place there last month. My young colleagues are convinced he is actively searching for your Fallujah *geniza.*"

"You think?" Abby asked.

"Let him finish!"

"Now here is the strange part, Sergeant. Your friends in the national police force have not arrested him, despite the fact that your military has put out an "arrest and detain" order. It seems that the national police are just watching him closely, for now. We think this means that they want our friend to lead them to the *geniza.*"

"The Iraqis don't have a clue about the *geniza.* And besides, this concerns us how?" Aaron asked with a bit of an edge to his voice.

"Actually, in a way, you led them to the *geniza.* The *Shin Bet* boys and girls believe that someone in Iraqi intelligence recognized you at the press conference. That someone began to wonder why an American advisor to the Iraqi National Police Force was participating in a news conference about a great archeological find, on Israeli television. I cannot give you the specifics, but recent intelligence from Iraq reveals contact between Professor Carlson and the Fallujah District Police. It turns out that an Iraqi Police Major, your dear friend Abdel Wahab, is the one giving the orders. This concerns you Sergeant, because other than Major Wahab, you are the only other person who knows where the *geniza* is.

"Therefore, my government, with the support of your government, is requesting that you assist us in locating the *geniza* and retrieving its precious contents before our professor friend or the Iraqis take them. It would be good for us to remember that the provenance of the 'original Torah' discovery can only be strengthened by locating the *geniza* and removing the rest of its contents."

"When you say 'you' does your government include me in the search?" Abby's tone did not reveal her feelings on the matter. Malik had no time to give her an answer.

"This is nuts! It's bad enough that I have orders to return to my duties in Iraq. There is no way you and your buddies are going to bring Abby into harm's way." Keller was vehement.

"Sergeant, I understand and share your concern for the rabbi's safety, but we need her." Malik was almost pleading.

"Would it be OK if **I** decided whether I am going to risk my life? I appreciate your loving concern, Aaron. It's sweet. But I'm a big girl and I can make my own decisions. Our recent engagement notwithstanding, I am still going to make my own choices--with your counsel and advice, of course--but they will still be my choices!" Abby was having a tough time keeping her voice down to a level where the other diners would not pay attention. Her angry whisper was beginning to turn heads.

"Why do you need Abby?" Aaron was puzzled.

"Yes, why do you need me?"

Sensing that he had at least achieved a modest level of interest in his pending operation, Malik began to make his case. "Let me count the ways."

Late on the morning of their last day in Israel, an agency car had been sent to take them back to Haifa. Malik came up to the penthouse. Aaron and Abby stood in a close embrace in their suite, trying to make the moment last forever. Malik was treating Abby and Aaron as his own children, alternating hugs with unsolicited marital advice. The trio had mild hangovers, so the embraces had the effect of keeping them steady, at least for the moment.

"It's time," Aaron said without conviction

"Yeah, it's time." Abby pulled him to her for one last kiss.

Abby's cell phone rang with the University of Michigan fight song blaring away.

"Did you have to put that on the max?"

"There is no ID on this call."

"It might be Omar or Rafi. It is unlikely that their calls would be identified. Go ahead and answer it."

"Good morning, Abby. How are you and Sergeant Keller doing? I have been following with great interest and delight your adventures in Jerusalem."

Abby placed her hand over the phone and feverishly pantomimed to Keller that the caller was none other than Professor Carlson. Aaron motioned for her to continue the conversation while he went to the room phone and alerted the agents of the *Shin Bet* in the hotel.

"Professor Carlson? Where are you?"

"It does not matter where I am. What matters is where I shall be."

"And where is that?" Abby placed the call on speakerphone so Aaron could hear.

"I am working on transportation to a *genizah* site known well to Sergeant Keller. Have a nice life." Carlson disconnected.

Abby and Aaron looked at each other, shook their heads, and said in unison: "He's already in Fallujah."

EPILOGUE

DATE: In the Twentieth Year of King Artaxerxes of Persia, Corresponding to the One Hundred Forty-Second Year Since the Destruction of Jerusalem, In the Month of Tishri, The Seventh Month, On the First Day of the Month
TIME: First Light
PLACE: Jerusalem

When the seventh month arrived—the Israelites being settled in their towns—the entire people assembled as one man in the square before the Water Gate, and they asked Ezra the scribe to bring out the Sefer Torat Moshe with which the Eternal had charged Israel. On the first day of the seventh month, Ezra the priest brought the Torah before the congregation, men and women and all who could listen with understanding. He read from it, facing the square before the Water Gate, from first light until midday, to the men and the women and those who could understand; the ears of all the people were given to the Sefer Torah. [The Book of Nehemiah. Chapter 8 verses 1-3]

GLOSSARY

Abba – Hebrew – Father

Ach, Achim - Hebrew - Brother, Brothers

Adoni - Hebrew - My lord, sir, mister

Alte kocker – Yiddish Lit. old Fart

Amah – Hebrew – Unit of length equal to two hand spans

Bavlim – the Babylonians. Singular – *Bavli*

*Bei*t – Hebrew – Lit. House. Also, ancestral house, i.e., dynasty as in *Beit David*, the House of David.

Birkat Hamazon - Hebrew - A blessing over food, the grace after meals.

Bubbe meises, Yiddish – As used, Grandmother's fables

Chazer Stahl - Hebrew and Yiddish- A pig stye

Chevre – Hebrew – idiom –[My] friends

Chotein - Hebrew - Father-in-law

Cohein - Hebrew - (Cohanim) – Priest (s)

Cohein Hagadol – Hebrew – Title: The great or high priest.

Dati - Hebrew-Orthodox

Emah – Hebrew – Mommy or mother.

Drash - Hebrew - The short form of *midrash.* A lesson derived from a sacred text. A sermon.

Ephod – Hebrew – A rectangular cloth with a hole cut in the center, worn as an over garment.

Eretz Yisrael. Hebrew – Lit. The Land of Israel. A traditional Jewish way to describe the territory without reference to the modern State of Israel.

Galil – Hebrew for Galilee. Area of Northern Israel from Haifa in the west to the Sea of Galilee in the east.

Genizah – A space set aside in a synagogue for the storage of texts which bear the sacred name of God and are no longer in regular use.

Giveret – Hebrew – Form of Address to women roughly equivalent to Miss, Ms or Madam.

Habibi – Arabic – My Friend.

Hatikvah - Hebrew - "The Hope" The national anthem of the State of Israel.

Hava Nagilah – *Israeli Folk song "Let us rejoice!"*

Herem – Hebrew – Excommunication.

Kalak - Babylonian - Large Rivercraft made from wood and inflated animal skins

Keter Shomron - Hebrew - The Crown of Samaria - Fictional group of Samaritans

Kibbutzniks – Members of a Kibbutz, an Israeli collective farm.

Kippa – Hebrew – curved dome. Common usage is skull cap.

Kaddish - Hebrew - Aramaic Lit. Sanctification. A prayer recited in memory of the departed.

Levir - Hebrew - The person who is next of kin to a deceased male who has died before fathering a son. He is obligated to marry the man's widow. The first-born son of that union is considered in all respects to be the son of the deceased.

Mamzer – Hebrew. Person born of a prohibited relationship. May only marry a person of identical *Mamzer* status.

Mazel – Hebrew – Lit. Planet. Idiom – Luck

Melekh Shomron – Hebrew –Lit. King of Samaria.

Mezuzzah – Hebrew – Lit. Doorpost. Idiom – A box or container or small carved niche affixed to the doorpost containing scriptural passages.

*Migbaha*t – Hebrew- conical headdress of the Aaronide priesthood.

Mishegas – Yiddish meaning craziness.

Mishkan – Hebrew Lit. Dwelling. The Biblical Tabernacle of the Israelites in the wilderness described in the Book of Exodus

Mishna – Hebrew – Lit. Second teaching. A text of Rabbinic legal discussions from as early as the second century BCE.

Mitzuyan - Hebrew - Excellent

Mish-Mash - Yiddish - Something mixed-up

Mossad – Hebrew Lit. The Institute. The Israeli equivalent of the CIA.

N'shama – Hebrew – Spirit, soul.

Oi Vavoi - Hebrew, Yiddish An idiomatic exclamation, equivalent to "Oh my God."

Parasang – Hebrew, Aramaic Unit of distance measure equal to 8,000 Amot.

Parsa – Persian Unit of measure equal to four Roman miles.

Pehcha – Aramaic/Babylonian title of government official

Saba - Hebrew - Grandfather

Sabra – Hebrew – Idiom Lit. a prickly pear cactus, used to denote native born Israelis.

Savta - Hebrew - Grandmother

Savlanut - Hebrew - Patience

S'gan – Hebrew – Lit. Assistant. The full term is sgan l'cohein hagadol - the assistant to the High Priest.

S'gan Aluf – Hebrew. Military rank equivalent to Lt. Colonel.

Sefer Torat Moshe – Hebrew - Scroll of the Teaching, or revelation of Moses.

Shakran - Hebrew - Liar

Shammes – Hebrew Lit. The server. Person designated by synagogue leadership to attend to the maintenance of the synagogue and its contents.

Sharav – Hebrew – The name of a strong wind that comes out of the Arabian desert.

Sheol – Hebrew – Place name for the dwelling place of the dead.

Shin Bet – An acronym from two Hebrew letters standing for the words Shirutei Bitachon –security service. This is an arm of the Israeli Ministry of Defense charged with the prevention of terrorist attacks on Israeli soil.

Shomronim – Hebrew – Samaritans

Sofer – Hebrew - Scribe.

Taggim – Hebrew. Decorative crowns on certain Hebrew Letters in a Torah text.

Tallit – Hebrew – Fringed garment. A large one, sometimes referred to as a prayer shawl, is worn outside the clothing for worship and for traditional males a smaller one is worn as an undergarment with the fringes outside the clothing.

Tuches – ass - Yiddish from the Hebrew Tachat, lit. below or bottom.

Yasher koach- Hebrew – Lit. "Straight is [your] strength." Idiom –Well done.

Yeshiva Bochers?" – Yiddish/Hebrew phrase for rabbinical students.

Yibum - Hebrew - The ceremony designating the intent to fulfill the obligation of the *Levir*

Yimach Shemo - Hebrew - "May his name be erased." Usually uttered as a strongly felt curse.

DEAR READER

I never intended to write a novel. Teaching classes on the *TANACH*/the Hebrew Scriptures was a passion I could indulge in as a congregational rabbi and as an adjunct professor of Jewish philosophy at St. Louis University. But it was the heartfelt questions of my students in both communities that propelled me down the path of historical fiction.

Every course I ever taught on the Bible began with a careful explanation of the Documentary Hypothesis. The short version goes something like this. The Bible as we know it today is a library of sacred texts, written by a multitude of authors and assembled over a period of 2,500 years. My students were usually accepting of the non-divine authorship of the text. But the question I could not answer was "How did it all happen?"

Albert Einstein is said to have had a talent for creating stories that explained complex mathematical concepts. Perhaps that would be the way to explain the compilation of the sacred texts we know as the Bible. If I could imagine the circumstances that led to the writing of the Torah, perhaps that would provide an answer to the question.

Two books moved me forward, one non-fiction and the other fiction. The non-fiction book was *Surpassing Wonder* by Donald Aiken. He describes the process of sacred text authorship as "invention." Ancient authors and scribes took existing works of religious tradition and reimagined them or reworked them. Over time they would take on the patina of being "sacred". We would eventually lose track of their human authors.

The other book that inspired me was the fabulously popular thriller, *The DaVinci Code*, by Dan Brown. In a work of fiction, he conveys Catholic Church history. He reveals the existence of once sacred materials suppressed by the Church that most readers knew nothing about. For me, it was hard not to notice the obvious. Brown was teaching Bible in a work of fiction and readers could not get enough of it. It certainly sounded like a plan for me.

My book first appeared as a self-published work, *The Ezra Scroll*. It was costly to produce and, now with hindsight, badly in need of editing. But it was out there. I had fans who kept prodding me for the next book. One of those fans was a rabbinical school classmate of mine, Donald Gerber. Donald is a natural salesman. He sold me, at the time of its first appearance, that the *Ezra Scroll* was a worthy effort, even a movie deal. He talked the book up every chance he got, to anyone who would listen.

One of those chances was a case of mistaken identity. Cruising the web, Donald took notice of the Newhouse Creative Group website. It caught his eye because he was a native of Syracuse and was familiar with the great philanthropy of the I.E. Newhouse family. He called the contact number on the NCG website and spoke with Keith Newhouse. He spoke with Keith Newhouse at length and convinced him to give the "second" book a fair look. As it turned out, Keith was definitely interested. Keith's dad, NCG author Mark Newhouse became my new editor. Under Mark's able guidance, it became a three-part thriller **The Search for the Sacred Scroll**. Mark helped in restructuring the *Ezra Scroll* and edited the first two installments: *Book 1 Discovery Under Fire;* Book 2 *The Secret of the Crowns.* Book 3 *The Samaritan Bone Box,* was edited by Amaryah Orenstein. She did an amazing job of helping me to realize the full potential of the story.

As with Books 1 and 2, this third and final episode in the *SEARCH FOR THE SACRED SCROLL* series is a work of fiction. All of the characters are fictional, with the exception of the Prophet Ezekiel and the Priest/Scribe, Ezra. Motivations, thoughts, and emotions are rare in Biblical narratives. The process of imagining what is "between the lines" in a Biblical text is known in Jewish tradition as *midrash.* This is the inspiration for the story of Eliezer, Zadok, and their descendants.

The storage of religious documents in a *genizah* is a real custom of some Jewish congregations. The *geniza* in the al Jolan district of Fallujah is fiction. Pumbedita **is** the ancient name of Fallujah. As Pumbedita, the city was a center of Jewish life and culture in ancient Mesopotamia.

I hope that after reading this series you are motivated to learn more about this crucial time in the history of the Jewish people and the world of the Bible in all of its iterations.

Thank you,

Mark Leslie Shook

ACKNOWLEDGEMENTS

Amaryah Orenstein, editor of Book 3 came to this project with a willing heart and an open mind. She plunged right in to reading Books 1 and 2 so as to understand the scope of the narrative. She got it! Thank you, Amaryah for your inciteful recommendations. I may not have adopted all of them, but I realized that you had the best interests of the book at heart. On more than one occasion, you found loose ends that needed cleaning up. Any mistakes that went unaddressed are all on me.

Samantha Wendling joined the staff of Congregation Temple Israel a few years ago. Her sincere interest in the contents of *The Search for the Sacred Scroll*, prompted me to invite her to share her IT skills in managing the number of draft copies of the story in the Cloud. She even provided clever graphic design ideas for the cover of Book 2, *The Secret of the Crowns*. Thank you, Sam, for your honest opinions, commitment and technical expertise.

Mere words cannot express my gratitude to the **Saturday Morning Bible Study Class of Congregation Temple Israel in St. Louis, Missouri.** Each week, for thirty years, they have asked great questions. Their love for the Biblical text and its history continues to inspire and energize me.

When I began this project, I had the broad outlines of the story clear in my head. I did not have control over the little details that add realism to fiction. I engaged a smart internet-literate student, **Jerry Thomeczek** and sent him forth to locate the enriching details. He made the key connection between modern Fallujah, Iraq and ancient Pumbedita, Babylon.

My colleague and friend, **Rabbi Jeffrey Stiffman** has distant family members in the modern Samaritan community. He assisted me in gathering materials on the Samaritan community now living in Israel. Their part in these stories is totally fiction.

Everyone needs someone who looks beyond. This is the person who sees the finished diamond beyond the uncut stone. I sent **Rabbi Donald Gerber** some early versions of this project. His unbridled enthusiasm kept me going forward. Our editorial conferences by the pool in Palm Desert, California gave me the sounding board I needed when plot dilemmas emerged. Thank you, Don for always being a true friend.

Thank you, Matthew Thomas for the two gorgeous maps which stand at the beginning of Books 2 and 3.

I am exceedingly grateful to **Keith Newhouse** of Newhouse Creative Group for taking this book under his wing and providing me with his father, **Mark Newhouse** as my first editor.

Most important of all, to **Carol**, my loving partner and wife of fifty-eight years, thank you for being my support and steady hand through all of the ups and downs of this project. I love you.

MLS

ABOUT THE AUTHOR

Mark Leslie Shook is, first and foremost, a teacher. He has been teaching his entire adult life. He taught junior high school science in his native city of Detroit, Michigan. He taught courses on Judaism at Stockton State College in New Jersey and, for twenty-four years, taught Jewish Philosophy at St. Louis University. Since 1987 he has been teaching *The Hebrew Scriptures* to adults in the St. Louis area from his position as Senior Rabbi and then Rabbi Emeritus of Congregation Temple Israel. All of these teaching experiences led him to writing historical novels based on Biblical literature.

Mark holds a Bachelor Degree in Anthropology/Near Eastern Studies, from the University of Michigan, a Bachelor of Hebrew Letters Degree, Rabbinic Ordination and a Master of Arts Degree in Hebrew Letters, and a Doctor of Divinity Degree, from the Hebrew Union College - Jewish Institute of Religion.

When he formally retired from the pulpit of Congregation Temple Israel in 2010, Shook rejected the "retired" label and chose instead to consider himself "repurposed." Police Chaplaincy became his focus. Serving as a chaplain for the St. Louis County Police Department since 1973 and the Creve Coeur, Missouri Police Department since 1995, he stepped up his game in 2010. St. Louis County Police appointed him as Chaplain Coordinator, managing a program of thirty chaplains serving in eight precincts within that department. In 2017 the St. Louis Division of the FBI invited him to serve as one of their three chaplains.

He and his beloved wife Carol have just celebrated their 58th wedding anniversary. They have two brilliant children and four exceedingly brilliant grandchildren.

FREE Book for Subscribing to The NCG Narrative

Subscribe to our free newsletter, The NCG Narrative, to immediately receive a **FREE** eBook from Newhouse Creative Group.

Be the first to learn about NCG's newest releases, get behind the scenes of NCG, enter NCG Narrative exclusive contests and giveaways, and much more!

Subscribe today at NewhouseCreativeGroup.com

Inspiring the readers and writers of today and tomorrow!

Visit NewhouseCreativeGroup.com for more books and other products from NCG Key and the rest of the Newhouse Creative Group family!

www.ingramcontent.com/pod-product-compliance
Lightning Source LLC
Chambersburg PA
CBHW060740180626
46819CB00001B/48